PERFECT EXCUSE

A. D. JUSTICE

SYNOPSIS

Who knew fighting for custody of an African grey parrot would be the perfect excuse to stay married?

Ryder King was always the one for me. He stole my heart in second grade, and I never imagined after seven blissful years of marriage, I'd give it back.

We made one tiny mistake by spending the night together during our separation period and the judge read all about it in the local gossip column. Okay, maybe it was two or three mistakes... but who's counting?

Instead of granting our divorce, the judge mandated us to marriage counseling. The only way to get out of our marriage without waiting another six months was if our counselor agreed we're all wrong for each other.

That's when the fun really started...

A probing therapist, a gossiper who knows all, and a few of my unmentionables on prominent display revealed all our secrets. Seems Ryder and I were both guilty of hiding vital truths from each other.

And what happened behind closed doors.... well, let's just say it's the stuff headlines are made of.

To all my author buds

PERFECT EXCUSE.

Copyright © 2021 A.D. Justice.

All rights reserved. No part of this book may be reproduced, resold, or transmitted in any form without written permission from the copyright holder, except by a reviewer who may quote brief passages for review purposes.

This is a work of fiction. Names, characters, places, and incidents are a product of the author's imagination. If the location is an actual place, all details of said place are used fictitiously, and any resemblance to businesses, landmarks, living or dead people, and events is purely coincidental.

The unauthorized reproduction or distribution of a copyrighted work is illegal. Criminal copyright infringement, including infringement without monetary gain, is investigated by the FBI and is punishable by up to five years in federal prison and a fine of $250,000.

All copyrights are held by A.D. Justice and have not been transferred to any other individual. Sharing or posting of this material in any group is considered copyright infringement and *will be* reported to the authorities. Criminal and civil charges will be pursued for damages.

CHAPTER 1

Olivia

"*Hide in the closet. Quick.*"

I hit replay and the incriminating phrase fills the room again. With an intentional glare at Ryder, I exit the app and dramatically lock my phone. "Care to explain how she learned to say that?"

"You really don't want me to explain it, Liv. This is all your fault, and you know it." Ryder points his finger at me with a jab in the air.

"My fault? How is any of this *my* fault?" If looks could kill, I'd be a widow instead of an estranged, soon-to-be former wife.

"Are you effing kidding me right now? You can't be serious." Ryder huffs and shakes his head.

His brows furrow, causing a crease to form between his eyes. I've only warned him a million times over the last seven years he'll cause a permanent wrinkle to appear there one day if he keeps making that face.

"I give you the master of the English language, ladies and gentlemen. He's always so articulate in describing his thoughts and feelings." With a flick of my wrist and an exaggerated roll of my eyes, I effectively end the negotiations.

Again.

Our mediator sighs heavily, then drops his forehead to the table. But even his muffled voice can't hide his irritation. "You two will be the death of me. I'm retiring to Tahiti the moment your divorce is final."

"Believe me, George, I feel your pain."

He rolls his head to the side to peer up at me from his partially prone position. His right eyebrow arches upward as his gaze changes from irritation to disbelief. "If I didn't know better, I'd think you're fighting to *stay* married instead of fighting to be apart."

"You *do* know better than that."

"You're crazy, George."

Ryder and I spit out our responses at the same time. Our matching intensity catches us off guard momentarily, followed by a pregnant pause when our eyes connect for the first time during this mediation session. When I stare into his sea-green eyes, I get lost there. It's an automatic response my body can't seem to shake.

"That's the first time you've both shut up over the entire past hour. Clearly, I have no clue what I'm talking about. Same time, same place, next week?" George sits up and folds his arms across his body, waiting for one of us to break free of the trance.

I'm the first to look away as I drop my gaze to the unsigned divorce papers in front of me. "Sure. Why not. Maybe Ryder will realize he has no business asking for joint custody sometime in the next seven days."

Before my almost ex-husband can reply, I snatch up the papers, push away from the table, and storm out of the room. The mediation process drains the life out of me every time we meet. It's hard enough to avoid seeing Ryder in the small town of Mason Creek, Montana. Population not even three thousand people. Add to that our businesses are practically next door to each other, and it's not exactly easy to remain separated during our legal separation.

On my way to Queen's Unmentionables, my lingerie shop, I call my best friend, Faith, to vent my frustrations. At this point in the game, she expects my call and has already penciled it in her busy schedule as the owner of Serenity Salon.

"Let me guess. You're still married." Faith doesn't bother to offer a greeting when I call anymore. She simply gets straight to the point.

"Yes, I'm still married. At this rate, I'll be an old wrinkled woman before my divorce is final. The truth is, I'm exhausted after rehashing the same argument every week for the last several months because we can't come to an agreement on the custody arrangement. We both refuse to sign the papers until we're completely satisfied with the terms."

"Liv, that's never going to happen. You and Ryder love her equally, so it's only natural neither of you wants to concede. I mean, you're already losing each other as it is." Faith understands loss better than most, and she tries to help me deal with the effects of mine every time we talk. "Maybe the underlying reason you two are fighting so hard is because you both need something to hold on to after all the years you've been together. Being alone is hard, especially when you're used to having someone around."

Her insight quickens my soul and steals my breath, making my steps falter until I stop and lean against the back wall of Wren's Café. She didn't say it to hurt me, of that I have no doubt, but the implications cut deep. Is all this bickering our way of keeping a part of our marriage alive so we don't feel so alone? Every day, I realize something small that makes me miss Ryder, but our irreconcilable differences are... irreconcilable. We reached this point in our relationship for a reason, or rather, for many minor reasons that all add up to an unresolvable large one.

"Maybe you're right, Faith. Even if Kiwi didn't hear that phrase from him and his extracurricular activities, Ryder and I are on completely different paths in life. We want different things, and our goals are too important for either of us to compromise. No matter how much we loved each other, we couldn't make the most vital parts of our relationship work. Maybe there's no love left between us now. Maybe we're simply more afraid of being alone than anything else." Merely saying the words out loud drives a knife deep into my heart.

"What in the world are you talking about? That's not what I said or meant at all. You and Ryder are so obviously still in love with each other, it's sickening. Even a blind person can see it. You're just both stubborn as hell and you're trying to hold on to a sliver of anything that keeps you together. If you two would only admit that to yourselves, you'd find a way to work through the rest of your shit together."

"What makes you think we're doing this to stay together, Faith? What proof do you have of any of it?

We can't get along anymore, and our life goals are the exact opposite. Given that, there's no way either of us will ever be happy together."

"Olivia Anderson-King, you've dragged your divorce out the last seven months over custody of a bird. A pet *bird*. I'm not stupid, sweetie. You're not fooling anyone around here but yourself. You and Ryder haven't let go of each other any more than you've let go of Kiwi. She's a great bird, don't get me wrong, but you've allowed this to go way too far. Even your mediator has threatened to leave town every week for the last six months because you two drive him crazy."

"I can neither confirm nor deny George may be in need of a vacation in Tahiti."

She chuckles. "A permanent vacation. You don't have to confirm or deny anything. We live in the smallest town in Montana. Everyone knows everything within minutes of it happening."

"You're right. Sometimes they know what's coming before anything even happens. The grapevine grows too fast around here."

"You should think about that fact. Don't you think everyone would know if Ryder had someone on the side? He may as well put his personal business on a billboard in the middle of the town square because everyone would be talking about him.

"All kidding aside, think about what you really want. Listen to your heart, not your pride. If you can't see your future without Ryder in it, you're making a huge mistake. I don't want you to regret this for the rest of your life."

"Thanks for always looking out for me, my bestie. I'm so glad you moved back here. Our long-distance relationship just wasn't working for me."

"I missed you too. But no matter where I am, I'm always here for you."

We disconnect as I walk into my store. Annie's behind the counter, already checking out one customer this morning, while Jasmine is on the sales floor, helping another. When I first opened this store, I doubted I'd have any customers who would dare to use the front door. My shop is filled with lingerie that would make Agent Provocateur blush, and I was sure this small town wouldn't accept my creativity with open arms.

"How'd it go today?" Annie turns her attention to me as the customer turns to leave.

"The same as every other time we've tried to come to an agreement."

"George threatened to quit again?"

"He said he's retiring to Tahiti today." I shrug one shoulder as the corner of my mouth lifts. As much as I hate going to these mediation sessions, George's quick wit at least provides some entertainment.

"Word around town is George didn't have gray hair before he started your divorce negotiations." Annie can't hide the enormous smile splitting her face in two. She loves busting my chops every chance she gets.

"George is a hundred and seven. He's had gray hair since I was a kid." We laugh together, and it feels good to release a little tension.

To everyone else, I'm fine.

As far as the town's wagging tongues know, I'm eager to get this divorce finalized and move on with my life without Ryder.

But what I know is, some days my heart and my head have a hard time getting on the same page.

Jasmine joins our no-progress-divorce party with a smirk. "Don't look now, but Mr. King is taking a leisurely stroll past the shop. Why do you suppose he's taking this route to his store?"

"He's just going by Java Jitters to get his caffeine fix before he goes to the jewelry store." With the utmost betrayal, my eyes land on Ryder as he walks past the front picture windows.

His jeans glide over his legs with every step, mesmerizing me until I forget I'm openly gawking at him. He has always had this effect on me. The way the denim hugs his thighs also can't be missed. But it's the view from behind that makes every female in town salivate over him. His thick brown hair, mesmerizing green eyes, and sexy smile are all equally lethal. We've known each other since second grade, but every passing year he becomes more handsome and better filled out. Unfortunately, his good looks can't fix what's wrong between us.

It's unfair, honestly, how he ages so well, like a fine wine. All I see when I look in the mirror is a shriveling prune.

That was one of the many fights that tore us apart. My body's internal clock reminds me every day how time is running out if I want to have kids. His clock only reminds him it's time to leave this sleepy little town and experience the great wide world, sans children, before we grow old and become permanent fixtures. It's as if we woke up one morning, realized we're moving full steam ahead in opposite directions, and what we wanted out of life can't be found in each other.

"It's almost scary how well you know him." Annie watches him walk into the coffee shop, as I predicted.

"I'm not so sure about that anymore." She doesn't hear my reply, but then I didn't intend for her to. I used to be so sure about us. But now the seed of doubt has been planted, and it's trying to take root.

But what hurts the most is we didn't grow apart.

We didn't stop spending time together. An offhand comment about turning one of the bedrooms into a nursery sparked a war, and neither of us will agree to a ceasefire. The sudden and abrupt change in the dynamics of our marriage created rifts and fissures in the very fabric that kept us together. One day, my entire world revolved around Ryder. The next day, he was torn from my hands.

At least it felt as if everything changed overnight.

The straw that broke the proverbial camel's back was when Kiwi started repeating the incriminating phrases. I know she didn't learn them from me, but Ryder insists she didn't hear them from him either. But then, of course he would counter and deny. Faith's words keep replaying in my head though. This place is too obsessed with gossip. Any infidelity would get back to my ears within seconds.

Hindsight may be twenty-twenty, but I've replayed our conversations throughout our years together while I've been alone the last seven months. I can't recall a single time Ryder ever said, hinted, or even inferred he didn't want a family. Turns out, I didn't know him anywhere nearly as well as I thought I did.

When my dream of having a big family shattered into a million useless pieces, something broke inside me.

I haven't figured out what that something is yet.

But I feel it all the way to my core, and it makes me feel incomplete. There's a part of me that's missing now, and I fear I'll never find it again.

Jasmine joins our conversation when the lady she was helping completes her purchase and exits the store. "Maybe I'm just a hopeless romantic, but I want you and Ryder to stay together. I've never met a couple who's more perfectly matched than the two of you are, Liv."

My best smile covers my face, but I don't feel it. "You're sweet, Jasmine. But it's time for a new perfect couple in this town. We need to start a matchmaking business and find your soul mate."

"No, let's not do that." She quickly shakes her head from side to side as her eyes grow wide with fear. "No more pet projects for you."

On cue, my pet bird hops from the top of her large cage onto my shoulder. "Hi, Kiwi, my sweet girl." She leans in to snuggle against my cheek as I scratch the side of her head.

"Hi, Momma."

Kiwi is an African grey parrot, one of the smartest birds in the world. This species is known for not only learning words and phrases but showing true comprehension in a conversation. Kiwi is exceptionally intelligent among her kind and has a sizeable vocabulary. Whether it's my imagination or not, I also like to think she senses when I'm sad and becomes even more affectionate than usual to comfort me.

She's the reason Ryder and I can't come to an agreement regarding our divorce. I won't sacrifice what's best for her just to make him feel better about turning our picture-perfect marriage into a second-rate stickman drawing.

"Kiwi missed you this morning. She kept asking for you." Jasmine watches Kiwi with a smile on her face. "She loves you so much."

"Daddy? Where's Daddy?" Kiwi's innocent question nearly brings tears to my eyes.

"He's at work, pretty girl."

"It still amazes me how smart she is." Annie leans her chin on her hands, watching us with thoughtful eyes.

"You know, these birds usually bond with one family member more than anyone else. But I think she loves Ryder and me equally. He and I alternated days bringing her to work with us from the first day we got her. They don't normally like change either, but we started this when she was young so it wouldn't be so jarring to her. Now I think she enjoys coming with us. But she looks for Ryder when we get home at night. She doesn't understand why he isn't there anymore."

Seems my impending divorce isn't easy on either of us.

CHAPTER 2

Ryder

A busy day in the jewelry store is more than what the doctor ordered to keep my sanity in check and stop the compulsive obsessing over the way my life is burning down around me. I can replace dead batteries and fix broken clasps with my eyes closed. After years of working in the shop with my parents, I'm able to perform most of the tasks with little effort. But the menial work keeps my hands busy and my mind from wandering. I need all the distractions I can get from the shitstorm that has become my life.

My day was as normal and dull, as usual, until a young man I've known since the day he was born came strolling in. Funny how a single ordinary encounter changes the mood on a dime.

"Hey, Josh. I haven't seen you in a while. Are you here to pick up a class ring or something?" I quickly scan my recent memories, trying to recall if I've seen an invoice for him.

"Hey, Ryder. No, I picked that up a long while back, when I was a junior in high school. Remember?" He walks over to the case with all the engagement and wedding rings, leaning over the glass with a permanent smile affixed to his face. "I'm starting college this fall, but I want to propose to Becky before I leave. We're going camping in the woods by the lake in a couple of weeks, and I'm planning a romantic, moonlit proposal on the old bridge out there."

His proclamation is like a knife to my chest. "You mean at the old Davis bridge?"

"Yeah. I know it's cheesy and overrated, but Becky thinks Henry Davis made the most romantic gesture in the history of the world when he built that bridge for his wife. So, I thought since he paved the way, I'll follow his lead." Josh shrugs like it's no big deal, but I know better.

"Just don't get caught camping on private property. They may not appreciate your squatting on their land." I chuckle, but there's no sincerity behind it. I'm simply doing my best to keep breathing at the moment. It'd be rude to keel over while my customer is picking out an engagement ring for his girlfriend. "Do you know what size ring she wears?"

"Actually, I do. While she was out shopping with a couple of her friends, I went by her house and had a talk with her parents. Her dad gave his blessing, provided we have a long engagement and we both finish college. I promised him we would, so her mom is secretly helping me make all the arrangements. They want to throw us an engagement party in a few weeks, assuming she says yes. You're invited, of course." Josh stops talking when the one ring to rule his world jumps out at him.

"That's the one. Right there." He pokes the glass with his finger. "Third row down, fifth one from the right."

"You have great taste, Josh." His particular choice is a variation of the one I created specially for my wife. This conversation is hitting a little too close to home for my comfort.

The bridge.

The moonlit night.

The romantic gesture.

The unique ring.

The end.

After verifying the ring size he needs against the ring in the display case, I give him my word to have it resized and ready to pick up in a week. Putting his heart out on the line for Becky potentially to stomp on is nerve-wracking, even if he's reasonably sure she'll accept. If I can help alleviate some of his stress by getting his order to him earlier than usual, it's worth the extra work.

When Josh leaves the store, I settle back in my office chair, run my hands through my hair, and stare at the ceiling. Memories come rushing back, overflowing the dams I've built in my mind like a swollen river during a flood. This isn't at all how I pictured my life would be when I was Josh's age.

That was the first sucker punch—the one I didn't see coming. When he said he was going off to college in the fall, I realized how quickly my life is slipping away. Though I've watched him grow up his entire life, nearly two decades have passed, but I'm still stuck in this small town. Now I can't leave until my divorce is final.

Divorce. A word I never dreamed would apply to me.

It's been several days since our last mediation session and I'm not anxious to repeat last week's disaster... or the week before that, or the week before that. Just as I sit up and lean forward, Liv walks past my shop on the other side of the road. I recognize the bag she's carrying. It's food from Wren's Café. We've gotten takeout from there enough for me to know exactly where she's been.

When she sits down at the picnic table, I'm surprised when a man sits down across from her with a matching bag. They spread the contents out on the table and begin sharing a meal together.

What is she doing? Is she... is she on a *date*?

Is my wife actually cheating on me?

I pretty much dismissed what Kiwi repeated because I thought I knew Liv better than that. She's always been the truest and most loyal person I've ever known.

But I can't deny what I'm witnessing right now.

She's eating with another man out in the open where everyone else in town can see what she's doing.

Who the hell is he? Scratch that. I don't care who he is. He's about to find out who I am when my fist connects with his mouth.

My hand is on the doorknob, ready to jerk the door open, before I realize I've crossed the entire length of my store. Then the truth smacks me across the face. She isn't cheating on me because she isn't mine anymore. Our divorce isn't final, but that's only because we're still arguing over custody arrangements. If we'd agreed to the mediator's suggestion six months ago, our divorce would've been finished already and we wouldn't be in divorce purgatory.

This is something I'll have to get used to seeing until I move away from here. She's still young and wants to have a big family. Her need to have several babies and my desire to experience the world, while I can, put us at odds. Children would tie us down and we'd never get out of this small town. Most of her friends have at least one baby, and that only increases her desire to have our own as soon as possible.

I just can't do it. I can't tie myself down while I'm still young enough to enjoy life. That's my story and I'm sticking to it... as far as everyone else knows.

Since that family she's set on having won't be with me, someone else will be more than willing to give it to her. While staring holes through my wife and her male companion, I calm down enough to realize who he is. Canaan Collins. He's a carpenter who moonlights as a Mason Creek volunteer firefighter. He's only a year older than Liv and me, making him the perfect candidate for her. The ink isn't even dry on our divorce yet. In fact, since neither of us has relented on our demands, there is no ink to dry.

A knock on the glass in front of my face draws my attention.

"Are you going to let me in or what?" Grayson, my best friend, smirks at me from outside.

"Or what." My deadpan response only makes him laugh as I turn the doorknob and let him in.

"Were you just stalking your wife?" He's teasing, but I'm busted nonetheless.

"Ex-wife," I shoot back.

"Not yet, she isn't. You still have time to fix this foolishness." Grayson turns to face me with his fists planted on his hips. It's the ultimate dad-stance. Not that he uses it on the two little girls who have him wrapped around their little fingers, but I can see him staring down any boy who shows up on his doorstep in a few years.

"We're at a stalemate and you know it. We can't fix this when we want to take two completely different paths in life. It doesn't matter how much I may or may not love her if we can't agree on where our lives are going."

"May or may not, my ass. You looked like you wanted to kill Canaan just now. You've known him your whole life." Grayson steps back to the window to get a better look at them. "Although, I can see why you're jealous. He's tall and fit. He has to be, though, to pass the physical tests as a volunteer firefighter. Working as a carpenter also helps keep him in shape. He's remained single all these years, so he wouldn't bring any baggage to the relationship. To top it all off, he's a genuinely nice guy. Come to think of it, Liv and Canaan would make a good couple."

"The fuck they would. How can you even say that?

She doesn't belong with anyone but me. Never has. Never will." My temper flares at the mere thought of any other man touching my wife. "Don't you dare go back to the firehall and put that shit in his head."

Grayson turns his head to look at me over his shoulder, and a knowing grin crawls across his face. I walked right into his trap without even looking for a trip wire first. "That was your gut reaction, Ryder. The first thought that came to your mind was Liv is *your* soul mate. She's sitting right there, living, breathing, flesh and blood, *alive*. You are making the biggest mistake of your life, but you don't even see it."

"Gray, I don't want kids. Your kids are great, and I love them with all my heart, but that's not what I have envisioned for the rest of my life. I want to leave this town and experience life outside of what we have available here. The closest I came to having any kind of adventure was when I went off to college, and that wasn't even out of state. I feel like I'm suffocating here—in this shop I never wanted to take over and in this town I never wanted to stay in."

"You think my kids keep me from living my best life? They *are* my life, Ryder. I had the same thoughts of leaving and becoming some big shot something-or-other at one time. But there's nothing I'd take over the life I have now. Being with my family is enough adventure for me, and they're all I need. I don't know why I get the feeling something else is up with you."

"Did you come here for a reason, other than trying to convince me to embrace the domestic life?" I arch one eyebrow, knowing damn well Grayson wouldn't stop in just to give me shit about my impending dissolution of marriage.

"Yes, as a matter of fact, I'm here as a customer today. Since the customer is always right..." His voice trails off as he walks to the counter and starts browsing the keepsake necklaces. Grayson has four-year-old twin girls, Harlow and Hayden, who are the center of his universe. Everything he does is for those two since his wife died. "I'll take two of these locket necklaces."

I don't have to ask why he wants them because I already know. The more the girls look like their mother, the more he wants to capture the resemblance. He'll put their pictures side by side in the lockets and save them for when the girls are a little older. After securing the necklaces in boxes I reserve for special clients, I hand him the bag.

"Any big plans tonight?" I know the answer before I even ask, but I can't let the moment pass.

"Same as every other night." He walks to the front door and stops with his hand on the knob.

"We really need to get out more." I shake my head,

knowing there are only so many places we can go around here.

"Ryder, you really need to get a new line. I'm heading home now. Have fun with Kiwi tonight."

"I don't have her tonight. She's with Livvy this week."

"Well, that makes more sense. You're alone, and you hate that. Enjoy your brooding time while stalking your wife. Huh, would you look at that? Liv and Canaan are feeding each other cake at the picnic table across the street." Grayson yanks the door open and makes a quick exit as I scurry to the window.

Sure enough, I arrive just in time to see Canaan drop a small piece of cake into Liv's open mouth. What in the actual fuck is going on?

Now I definitely need a drink or ten.

After a quick glance at my watch, I decide it's near enough to closing time for me to lock up the store and take a stroll past the picnic area. Olivia glances toward me when movement catches her eye, then does a double take when she realizes it's me. The same flash of pain crosses her face when our eyes meet. It happens every time, and every time it hurts me all over again.

"Hey, Ryder. How's it going?" Canaan asks casually.

"Good. How are you, Canaan?"

"Can't complain, man. It's a warm summer day.

We have awesome scenery, and I'm helping a gorgeous lady taste-test different flavors of wedding cake. Doesn't get much better than this." He smiles, but there's no hint of aggression or superiority in his demeanor. He's the same Canaan I've always known him to be—laid back and easy-going.

"Who's getting married?" I turn my attention solely on Liv, watching for the usual telltale signs that show on her face when she tries to hide something from me.

"My friend, Miranda, from college. You remember her, right? She wants to get married here in Mason Creek, so she asked me to help her plan it. I ran into Canaan in the bakery when I went to pick up the samples. He offered to help me carry everything, then he stayed so I wouldn't have to eat alone." The underlying message in her piercing gaze says so much more than her innocent words ever could.

"Yeah, yeah, I remember her. Sure. Why would she want to get married here?" My eyebrows draw down instinctively.

"Man, are you kidding? People love this little town. It's perfect for a romantic wedding. It's also the ultimate honeymoon spot because it's insulated from the outside world. Someone could make a killing as a wedding planner around here." Canaan pops another piece of cake in his mouth, then his eyes fly wide open.

"This is the one, Liv. My sister outdid herself when she baked this one."

Without giving her a chance to respond, he pops the chunk into Liv's mouth. Her reaction is equally enthusiastic as she quickly nods in agreement. "Oh my gosh, you're right. This one is delicious. I'll tell Miranda we've found the perfect cake for her reception."

Seeing their interaction up close and personal, I realize this is all completely harmless. They're friends, always have been, and that's all there is to it. Canaan helped her because I wasn't there to do it.

"Tell Miranda I said congratulations. I should get going now."

"Later, man," Canaan replies.

Livvy watches me for an extra second or two as I step back from the table, then I turn and keep walking toward my condo. The one I moved into when my marriage fell apart. The one I've grown to hate more with each passing day. Kiwi is my only companion, but she's not there all the time. Even when she is with me, she asks where Liv is.

I fish my ringing phone out of my pocket and see Malcom's name on the screen. He's the mayor of our small town and a good friend to everyone.

"Hey, Malcom. What's up?"

"We're all going to Pony Up tonight, including you.

Grayson is intentionally avoiding my calls. Grab him on your way and make him join us. We can all use some time to unwind."

"Shit, you got that right. I'll do my best, but you know he's Mr. Mom now. It's hard to get him to leave the nest."

"Hog-tie him and drag him out tonight if you have to. We'll vouch for you." Malcolm laughs good-naturedly, but I promptly agree to do just that if I have to.

We disconnect as I turn the corner, and the sight in front of me immediately brings a huge smile to my face. Twin four-year-old girls have me in their sights before I can utter a single word.

"Uncle Ryder!" They bolt toward me as fast as their little legs can carry them.

I squat down and gather them both up in my arms at once, stealing kisses from each little beauty. "How are my girls? I've missed you."

"Fine. We're spending the night with Nana and Pop." Hayden leans in closer to whisper. "They let us have ice cream in the bed."

"What? That's not fair. I don't even get to eat ice cream in the bed." I feign a mad look and they both laugh at me, knowing all too well I'm only playing.

"Uncle Ryder, you can come have ice cream with

us tonight." Harlow puts her little hands on my cheeks and turns my face to look at her.

"Baby girl, I would love to, but I already have plans tonight. Can we make a date to do that next week? I'll bring the ice cream and we'll eat it in front of your dad."

"Yes!" They both squeal at the same time.

I chat with their nana and pop for a minute before turning my little sweethearts back over to their care. When I reach my place, I call Grayson.

"Hey, best friend o'mine. I know all about my girls staying with their grandparents tonight. That means you're home alone, wearing your prettiest apron and getting your Mr. Clean on. Change clothes. You're coming out to Pony Up with all the guys tonight. Both of us need this, and I'm not taking no for an answer."

He hesitates for a moment, then relents with a heavy sigh. "Fine. Pony Up it is. I'll meet you there."

CHAPTER 3

Olivia

"A bunch of us girls are going to Pony Up tonight to listen to music and throw back enough shots to make us all puke at the same time. You're going with me. The foot is down. I'll call Jasmine and ask her to come over and babysit Hope while we're out." I don't give Faith a chance to make up any excuses to stay home.

"You're so pushy and demanding. Fine. I'll go with you. But don't worry about asking Jasmine to keep Hope. I know she would in a heartbeat, but my mom is on kid duty tonight."

Faith and I talk a little while longer about our choice of outfits for the night and what time to meet at the bar. "Charlotte and Grady are acting as our official taxi service to and from the bar. I'm taking full advantage of our designated driver tonight."

"Tell me again how it's a girls' night out when the guys are always there." Her quick wit always makes me laugh.

"The men sit at a different table and watch from afar in case their women need anything. It's harmless, and in this case, it's also convenient. Grady will sip on water all night so Charlee can let loose. Tucker will watch Justine from the sidelines. All the while, they'll deliver shot glasses to our table so we can have fun. A couple of their friends will probably join them too."

"What if Ryder shows up? Will you be all right?"

"Sure, I'll be fine. All the alcohol will numb the pain, right?" Nothing else has worked so far, but a girl can still hope.

"You can't lie to me, Liv King. I know you better than anyone else in this town does. You could dive headfirst into a vat of tequila, but it wouldn't make you forget your first love."

"Normally, that would be true. But not tonight. For the next few hours, Ryder King doesn't exist."

We disconnect, then I walk toward the screened porch on the back of my house. Ryder and I converted it to a bird sanctuary soon after we brought Kiwi home. I lean against the doorframe and watch Kiwi before she knows

PERFECT EXCUSE

I'm there. One side of my mouth lifts in a cheerless smile as I reminisce about the care Ryder took in the layout of her new home. Every branch had to be in the perfect position. He placed multiple toys in various locations to keep her entertained. The room looks like a tropical jungle.

At the time, I remember thinking if he took such great care of our pet bird, one day he'd make a wonderful father.

"Hello." Kiwi leans over, putting her face directly in front of mine. Then she rubs her beak against my cheek. "Love you."

"I love you too, sweet girl." She's so affectionate, and she warms my heart when I've had a tough day.

"Is she gone yet?" Her voice lowers an octave or two as if she's trying to whisper, but the words cut through my heart like a hot knife through butter.

"She will be when I catch her, sweetheart. And her body will never be found."

That's it. I'm getting shit-faced tonight and I don't care who sees me. Rumors be damned.

If I have to suffer through this, at least I'll do it in style.

Pony Up is a great place, but it's not exactly the high-end bars my parents frequent when they visit New York City. The dress code is much more come-as-you-are than if-you-have-to-ask-you-can't-afford-to-get-in. I'm breaking the Mason Creek law tonight and wearing something unexpected.

On an uncharacteristic whim, Mom bought an outfit for me on one of her whirlwind world trips. It's the cutest pale blue strapless romper. The fabric belt hangs lower than the shorts, but that only accentuates my tan legs. Since we'll be dancing and drinking, I'll pair it with my Boho style toe ring sandals. I may never fall in love and marry again for the rest of my life, but I'll look damn good while not doing it.

I've prided myself on my fashion sense and being able to mix unexpected elements for several years now. My talent really blossomed when I was in college and finally found the confidence in myself to become bolder and more daring in my wardrobe choices. That eventually led to opening my own business after I graduated and moved back to my hometown.

Though I'm outgoing and friendly to everyone, I have a huge secret I haven't shared with anyone. Not even Ryder. Sometimes I wonder if withholding part of my life from my husband jinxed our marriage. It's too late to focus on the what-ifs and if-onlys everyone experiences in the aftermath of a broken relationship.

I push the pain aside and focus my attention on getting dressed to kill tonight. Faith asked about Ryder out of concern for me, and I played it off as well as I could. But I do think he'll show up at the bar tonight.

There are only so many places to hang out around here, and Pony Up is the best. Besides, he won't be happy sitting home alone.

Just as I finish dressing, the double tap of a car horn lets me know my ride has arrived. I rush to the window and see Charlee hanging out the passenger side window, waving an arm and yelling my name. "Liv, it's time to get our party pants on! Let's go, girl!"

I grab my small purse, just big enough to hold my license, credit card, and house key, and dash out the front door. "I'm so glad Justine sent up the flares so we can let off some steam tonight. It feels like I've been cooped up in a box for a year."

"You look *hot*. I may have to dump Grady for you before the night's over." Charlotte fans herself with a playful wink.

"I heard that," Grady grumbles from the driver's seat as I slide into the back. The smirk on his face as he turns to look at me over his shoulder betrays his serious tone. "Charlee's not leaving me for you, Liv, so don't get any ideas about my woman."

"Don't mess with me, Grady Jackson. You know how the people in this town love to gossip about me. I'll start a new rumor about Charlee and me, and I'll make it damn good. The one Hazel and Hattie started about you and me will be considered boring by comparison." The three of us burst out in laughter at the same time.

It wasn't funny at the time, but now that we're past the effects of the rumor mill, we can joke about it.

Grady and I have known each other basically since the day I moved to Mason Creek when I was a little kid. When Charlee joined the ranks of our town, she fit in so naturally, I would've thought she was born and raised here. He and I have never been anything more than friends. Ryder King has always held my heart in his hands. Deep down, I think everyone knows that, but the temptation to gossip is too much to resist. We swing by to pick up Faith, then head into town for a little dancing and a lot of drinking.

The music is jumping when we enter the bar, and the rhythm seeps into my blood immediately. I can't stop myself from dancing all the way to the table where Justine, Lenora, and Laken have claimed our spot. When Tucker sees us coming, he kisses Justine on the cheek, then meets Grady halfway. The men move to a table in the back to give the illusion of a separation between the boys and the girls, but we all know better. If any hot rod wannabe so much as looks at their women the wrong way, the guys will swoop in and put a stop to that shit immediately.

It's sweet how protective Tucker and Grady are of Justine and Charlee. The guys don't hover or smother them, but the ladies know they're well taken care of should they need anything at all. I don't show it, but I miss the security I felt when Ryder did the same for me. I'm strong and independent, always have been, but since we've been apart, I've realized there were so many small things I depended on him to do. Maybe I took those things for granted... took him for granted... assumed we were on the same page because I wanted a big family.

"Get out of your head." Faith leans over and speaks in my ear so no one else can hear. "We're here to have fun and forget our real-world problems, remember?"

"I'm trying." I nod and flash her a smile to show I'm here with her and not lost in a dream world.

"Come dance with me. The drinks should be ready by the time the song's over." Faith stands and pulls me up with her.

On the dance floor, I close my eyes and let the music take the lead. My hips sway with the beat, my legs move to the tempo, and my heartbeat keeps time with the cadence. Then I let go and allow the music take control. I feel others bump into me as they dance, but I block them out and stay lost in my own musical world.

When the song ends, Faith and I make our way back to the table and throw back our first couple of shots. "That was exactly what I needed. Thank you for coming out with me tonight."

"I'm so glad you didn't give me a choice." She

chuckles, then someone behind me catches her eye. I can't help but turn and see who it is.

"You little minx! You didn't tell me you have a crush on Mitch Collins."

"I don't." She denies it a little too quickly and forcefully.

"You do. I saw how you were just looking at him. You don't give men that look for no reason. You like him."

"There was no look. You're imagining things." She won't make eye contact with me.

"Faith Evans, I know what I saw, and you were the one who was imagining things. Very dirty, naughty, sexy things. It was written all over your face. Look how red it is now." When she playfully punches my arm, I only laugh harder. "You should come by my shop tomorrow. I've got just the thing to help make your fantasies come true."

"You know he won lunch with me when he bid on my basket at the festival. It was simply a sweet gesture on his part. Nothing more."

"Faith... the man bid a thousand dollars to win lunch with you. That's a little more than a sweet gesture. There's nothing wrong with you *appreciating* him in return. You can show him how much you're grateful for his bid while wearing one of my sexy, sheer bodysuits. It sparkles in the light and glows in very strategic spots in the dark." Even in the dim bar lighting, I can see her face turn fifty shades of pink from embarrassment.

"I'd rather talk about how we're going to fix this little hiccup between you and Ryder. You've made your point. We all know you're stubborn and crazy at the same time. Apparently, you've rubbed off on him because his crazy now matches yours. Admit you're miserable without him and be willing to compromise to save your marriage. If he was unable to father children, you wouldn't have divorced him." She pins me with her try-to-argue-with-me expression.

"We're not talking about that tonight because it's not happening, babe. But you're right, I would've stayed with him forever if he was unable to have kids. Except, he's not unable, only unwilling. I'm thirty, Faith. I've made concessions and waited this long. I'm not the only one who needs to cooperate here."

"All right, you two look like you're in a deep discussion down there." Justine yells at us from the other end of the table. "We'll have none of that shit tonight. Lock it up, ladies. We're here to have fun."

"You're absolutely right, Just. We need another round or two or ten of tequila shots to get this party started." I grab a passing waitress and ask her to hook us up with enough liquid courage to make us forget all our troubles.

When a full tray of shots appears before us, we all stand and take one in each hand, holding them up as a salute to everyone. Justine yells the countdown to the table, preparing everyone to drink our shooters at the same time. When she hits three, my eyes stray to the back of the bar as if they knew he was here before my brain had a chance to comprehend it.

Ryder's here, sitting with Grayson, Tucker, Grady, and Malcolm. His eyes are fixed directly on me, and a scowl covers his face. His drawn brows make him look more menacing than usual. His arms are crossed over his chest and his head is cocked to the side.

Damn, if he doesn't look even sexier tonight than ever.

CHAPTER 4

Ryder

"Every fucker in this place is looking at her."

I can't take my eyes off her. Her long blonde hair and blue eyes are eye-catching enough, but she's killing me with that one-piece outfit she's wearing. The strapless top reveals every inch of her slender neck and sexy shoulders. The shorts hang loose against her toned legs, swaying with her every movement as she walks and dances. From the moment she moved here, I've been caught in her spell. Tonight is no different.

Grayson is good enough not to say anything about my foul mood. We've been best friends long enough for him to know when to push the issue and when to let it go. I brood in our corner of the bar alone, while he and the other guys serve another tray of drinks to the ladies. They're here for harmless fun. My head knows that, but my heart can't bear the thought of some guy taking my wife home for a one-night stand.

When the men return to our table, they can't stop ribbing Grayson about the obvious connection he and Laken had during their brief interaction. He deserves another chance at love. After losing his wife, he's raising his twins alone. I've supported him every step of the way, but there's only so much a best friend can do to help. If he'd open himself up to the opportunity, he'd find so much more happiness.

On the other hand, I also understand why he's still hesitant after all this time. I've been apart from my wife for seven months and still can't get her off my mind. Even when the ink is dry on the papers and the dust has settled from the storm we've created, I'll always think of her as mine. There's not another woman in the world who can match Livvy in my eyes.

Hours pass as the ladies have fun dancing with each other, laughing, drinking, and talking with other friends. I join in the conversation at our table as best I can, trying not to be the downer of the group. Liv arrived with her best friend Faith, but Faith left earlier than the rest. My bet is she wanted to get home to her daughter.

"Liv said Charlee and Grady are giving her a ride

home tonight. Faith caught a ride with one of the ladies who works at her salon." Grayson knows exactly what's on my mind. Closing time is approaching quickly and my wife has to get home somehow.

"They're losing steam. I think it's time to wrap up this girls' night out. We should probably get them home now." Malcolm begins to push his chair back from the table when a feminine voice catches everyone's attention.

"Ry? Take me home?" Liv stands behind me, swaying on her feet from the number of shots she consumed tonight.

"Of course." I jump to my feet, slide my arm around her waist, and walk her out to my truck. Though I don't say it, I'm grateful she asked me over anyone else in the bar tonight.

I pour her into the passenger side of my truck and fasten the seat belt over her. It's a small town, but I won't take any chances when she's shown implicit trust in me. Besides, heading to our former shared home just outside the city limits where the countryside quickly takes over, there are any number of large animals we could encounter along the way.

She instinctively reaches for my hand when the truck begins to move. Then she leans her head against the headrest and closes her eyes, secure in the knowledge I'll keep her safe. As we drive along the familiar streets, I tighten my fingers around her hand and lift it to my lips. It's been too long since I've felt the warmth of her touch or enjoyed her sweet scent. She smells like honeysuckle after a spring rain.

She smells like home.

When I glance over at her as I pull into the driveway, I realize she's already asleep. She still hasn't released my hand, but I know she's too far gone to be alone tonight. I turn off the truck and quickly walk around to her side. She opens her eyes and looks at me when I unbuckle her seat belt and turn her legs toward me. I stop what I'm doing and meet her gaze.

She lifts her hand to cup my face, her palm lying flat against my cheek. She curls her fingers, scraping the tips across my stubble. "I've always loved playing with your beard."

The memories of how often she used to do that flood my mind, making me chuckle. "Yeah, babe, I know you do. You did it during our wedding and caused all kinds of rumors to fly around town."

"They were all just jealous bitches who wanted your beard for themselves." She slurs her words, but she says them with complete conviction.

"Yep, I'm sure that's what caused all the talk. It couldn't have been the way you were undressing me with your eyes during the ceremony." She puts her arm around my neck and I help her stand, keeping my hands on her waist long enough to make sure she's steady on her feet before I move again.

"I can't help it if your stubble reminded me how raw the inside of my thighs were." She grins mischievously.

My intentions were good. Get her home safely. Keep her out of the arms of some horny guy. Sleep on the couch in case she needs me tonight.

The road to hell is paved with good intentions.

Our bodies are perfectly aligned, and she's in my arms. She steps closer, closing any gap that remained between us, and I close the door with a flick of my wrist. Her arms tighten around me, her breasts press against my chest, and her warm breath tickles my ear.

"Take me inside, Ry."

"Babe, you've had a lot to drink tonight. I don't want you to regret this in the morning." I'm trying to be a good guy here, but she's making it very hard.

Very.

Very.

Hard.

"I'm not *that* drunk, Ry. You're not taking advantage of me. I'm inviting you in... to stay with me."

"You know I've never been able to turn you down, Liv. If you want me to stay tonight, I'm yours all night."

She leans back enough to look me in the eye, then her lips land on mine. Standing on the driveway under the light of the moon, I'm taken back to when we were dating. Sneaking around town, making out wherever we could find a private place, and hoping no one saw us. Tonight, I don't care who sees us. The entire town can walk by in a holiday parade and take pictures as far as I'm concerned.

Our kiss changes from a slow burn to a raging inferno in a split second. I step forward, pushing her back against the truck door, and lean my full weight against her. Her soft moans work me into a frenzy. I slide my hand down her body and lift her leg. She wraps it around me, using it to pull me in tighter. Loving her feels so natural to me, like second nature. Though I've tried my best to hide it from all the busy bodies around town, I've missed her in every way possible.

My lips trail down her neck, my teeth graze across the sensitive skin of her neck, and goose bumps flare out across her skin. She curls her fingers into a fist, gathering my shirt in her grip. I'm getting drunk on the taste of her and high on the sounds she makes.

"Ryder, if you don't take me inside right now, I'll tell everyone about the time we went skinny-dipping in the frigid waters of the blue hole, and your dick was so shriveled up you thought it would never come out of its warm shell again."

I chuckle against her skin, just above her collarbone. "Tell them whatever you want, babe. All your screams tonight will prove that's a lie, whether we're outside or inside."

"Now, Ryder. Right now."

"You're so demanding." I step out of her leg-hold and lift her off the ground, carrying her like a baby. When I reach the front door, a different metaphor pops into my head. I'm carrying her across the threshold, like she's my new bride, and now we're starting our lives together.

Our first stop is the couch, only because it's close and we're on the edge of the ignition point as it is. I put her down, and she hesitates only a moment, long enough to meet my gaze head-on. Her eyes convey her thoughts without speaking the words. She wants and needs this as much as I do. Seven months without the feel of her body connected to mine. Two hundred ten days without holding her in my arms. Five thousand forty hours since our world imploded when we hit an impasse.

But tonight, I'm leaving all that lost time in the past, and focusing solely on the present. I don't know what tomorrow holds, but I know I'm holding her all night tonight. When the back of her knees hit the couch, she tugs on her belt, and lets it fall to the floor. Then she pulls down the strapless top of her outfit, shimmies it over her hips, and steps out of it.

My libido instantly hits overdrive, and it takes all my restraint not to rush the moment. But since we haven't resolved anything that drove us apart, I'm not hurrying a single second of this interlude in our ongoing war. The chemistry between us has never been in question... only our ability to work out the irreconcilable differences we never knew we had.

Then she palms my cock through my pants and all semblance of rational thought flees from my mind. I push down on her shoulders until she sits on the couch, then I pull her legs to slide her to the edge. Her hooded eyes and ragged breaths urge me on. I stroke her core and watch with rapt attention as her eyes roll back in her head before closing. She leans against the back of the couch, arching her back and pushing her breasts toward me. With one hand I continue the ministrations that make her body shudder and slide the other up to accept the open invitation from her exposed breast.

When I press my thumb against her sensitive nub in small circles and squeeze her taut nipple simultaneously, she nearly vaults off the seat. She grabs my arms and digs her nails into my skin, struggling to contain her cries of passion. Intent on hearing those cries as loudly as possible, I increase the pressure and intensity until she can no longer hold back. Her entire body goes rigid at once before melting into a pile of beautiful skin and bones right before my eyes.

"That's one." I don't even try to hide the pride in my voice.

"Let's go for a record tonight. You up for it?" She arches one brow as she issues her challenge.

"You know damn well I am. The real question is if *you* can handle it." I move closer and drop my head between her thighs. "You'll probably want to hold on to something."

My mouth covers her core, my tongue laps up her wetness, and my fingers delve deep inside her to stoke the fires even more. She writhes under my attentions, simultaneously pulling my hair and squeezing my head with her legs. When another scream breaks free, despite her best attempts to hold it at bay, I glance up at her with a sly, seductive grin.

"And that's two. I wonder how many more I can wring out of you."

"Holy hell, I don't know. But if you touch me again right now, I may just die right here on the spot."

"Yeah? Let's see." Before my threat registers, I dive back in and suck her clit into my mouth.

"Oh. Shit. Ry. Ooohhhh." She barely manages to get the words out before my voracious appetite returns. What follows is a series of incoherent and senseless words followed by feral, guttural sounds... before that glorious squeal makes another appearance.

"Three. Seems I'm on a roll, and you're extra sensitive tonight. I could use this to my dark gain and hold you hostage as my sex slave." I waggle my eyebrows at her.

"Don't make idle threats to me, Ryder King. Only come at me if you have a solid plan." I've missed the teasing smirk on her face. It's been way too long since we've felt at ease with each other.

"I'm an evil genius. I'll show you my master plan." Her eyes remain glued to me as I remove every shred of clothing on my body. When I take my place in front of her again, her tongue emerges, sliding across her lips in a slow, seductive taunt. "Keep looking at me like you want to eat me alive, babe. You'll get your wish in just a second."

"A second is too long to wait."

She pulls me to her, and our mouths clash in hungry need. Her hands glide across my back, scoring my skin with her nails. I'm completely lost in this embrace, but I need to see her face before we move to the next level. After I break our kiss, I slide my hand behind her neck to keep our eyes locked. Then I thrust inside her to the hilt, holding her attention with an invisible tether neither of us can break.

She sucks in a breath with a hiss during my sensual intrusion, then she begins lifting her hips to meet me. With a slight circular movement, she grinds against me as I repeatedly pull back and push forward into her.

Sweat covers our bodies, glistening off the moonlight that illuminates the living room through the large picture window. She calls out my name more times than I can count because I'm too focused on delaying my own pleasure.

I don't want this night to end.

However, all good things must come to an end, and that end is together as we reach the highest of highs. Her inner muscles tighten their grip around me as her final climax rips through her body, pulling me along with her as we tumble over the edge as one. We clean up, then crawl in the bed together. She's asleep in my arms in under a minute, but I'm still awake, watching her for as long as I can keep my eyes open.

Our problems didn't magically disappear tonight. We're still at odds with our expectations, both too stubborn to give up. But our love hasn't diminished. Time and distance can't change how we feel about each other. The lull of sleep eventually takes over my senses and I succumb to the darkness behind my eyelids.

Sometime before the morning light begins to peek over the mountains, I'm awoken by the most divine sensation. Liv is under the covers, situated between my legs, and working all kinds of mischief with her tongue and lips. My hands instinctively move to her head, fisting her hair between my fingers, and gently guiding and encouraging her to move faster. When I don't think I can hold back any longer, she straddles me and takes me fully inside her. As she bounces up and down on my cock, I struggle to maintain my composure. Then I reach forward and stroke her clit, giving her the extra attention she needs to reach that spot again.

"Now, Ryder. Oh my God, right now!"

Watching her head loll backward, the expression of sheer ecstasy on her face, and her body lose all muscle control is the most beautiful sight I've ever seen. She slumps forward, puts her head on my chest, and falls asleep while lying on top of me. Without moving too much, I pull the covers over her, then wrap my arms around her back.

CHAPTER 5

Olivia

"Daddy! Daddy!" Kiwi wakes me, screaming for Ryder. Again. She misses her daddy, and she misses us being together.

She's usually in her luxurious suite with the blackout shades drawn so she'll sleep in, but I left the door open since I knew I'd be away most of the night. Keeping her cooped up too long isn't good for her, even though she has an extra-large enclosure. She needs the human interaction and bonding time every day. Though I can't pry my eyes open yet, I'm certain she's perched above my head on my headboard.

My brain is still foggy from the copious amount of alcohol I drank over the span of several hours last night. I was noticeably tipsy when I left Pony Up, but not what I'd consider drunk. I've only been truly drunk twice in my life, and both times resulted in bowing to the great porcelain throne, so I don't make that mistake anymore.

"Daddy, I love you. Love you, Daddy." Kiwi's louder and more animated than usual this morning. It doesn't help that she's now sitting on my head, bobbing up and down and walking around in my hair.

But something is amiss underneath my head.

The only fact I'm certain of is I'm not lying on my pillow. There's something underneath me that's both hard and soft, comfortable and prickly, and warm and lean. A rash of memories rushes back to me, flooding my mind with vivid images all at once. I squeeze my eyes shut and scrunch my face, knowing exactly what I'll find when I muster the courage to look.

"Daddy. Home. Daddy. Home." She bounces around, repeating the words in a singsong voice. She's thrilled to have him back, and it breaks my heart because I know he'll leave again soon. Then she'll ask where he is, and we'll start this vicious cycle all over again.

"Shh, sweet girl. We have to be quiet. Come here and give Daddy some love." Ryder's voice is soft, trying not to wake me in case Kiwi hasn't already succeeded. When I feel him lift her from my head, I know I can't delay the inevitable any longer.

I raise my head, cross my arms on his chest, and and rest my chin on them. It's not the most comfortable position, but it's the safest with the way our limbs are entangled under the covers. "She doesn't know how to be quiet."

He smiles, but it doesn't reach his eyes. The truth of our current situation has already taken root in his mind. He's being polite and considerate because I was still asleep. Or because I'm still on top of him. Maybe because he's in my bed and in my house. Regardless, all the above used to be his too. The house, the bed, and me. We have a hell of a mess to extricate ourselves from this morning... all before the automatic coffee maker kicks on.

"Morning, sleepyhead."

Maybe I'm overanalyzing our early morning interactions, but I take special note of how he didn't say "*good* morning."

"Have you been awake long?"

"Not too long. Kiwi landed on me and woke me up. I tried to keep her quiet, but she's just too excited." He nuzzles her, rubbing his cheek against hers. They both look so content.

He tries to hide it, but I notice the small differences in his demeanor when he looks at me. His guard instantly goes up, and his heart hardens. We've known each other for so long that we finish each other's sentences and share the same thoughts. I don't need him to say the words out loud for me to sense what he's feeling. Reading his demeanor is an involuntary reflex after all the years we've spent together.

Maybe he's protecting himself, but it also feels a lot like he's shutting me out. Just like he did the day I wanted to talk about having a family, but he wanted to clam up regarding the whole topic. There was no discussion or consideration for my feelings. Just an open-and-shut case of not being tied down to the small-town life he hates.

The problem with that scenario, which he doesn't seem to realize to this day, is the life he says he hates is, and has been, our entire life together.

That was when the hurtful realization hit me that nothing in our life made him happy. Our businesses, our home, our marriage, and our little family were all the exact opposite of what he wanted for his future. What we had together was our small-town life—the very one that wasn't good enough for him. This life wouldn't work anywhere else. My lingerie shop would be dwarfed by the larger department stores, as would the jewelry store he bought from his parents when they retired early. Anywhere else, we'd be stuck in the nine-to-five grind of corporate life, miserable and looking for a way out.

Another realization hits me out of the blue. I've

been lying on him way too long. If I move now, it'll be obvious. If I don't move, it'll be even more awkward than it already is. When I move, I don't know how to unwrap my leg from his, or the sheet that's now oddly twisted around both of us.

There's no easy way out of this mess, so I fling myself to the side as hard as I can, rolling off him in one fluid motion. Except... the covers don't stay in place. In fact, they all come with me. Every. Single. Thread. Leaving Ryder completely nude beside me, with no way to cover himself. Trying my best to play it off, I roll again, right off the bed. As I walk away with the sheet twirled around my right leg, I call over my shoulder to Ryder.

"Coffee?"

"Um, yeah, sure."

I stroll past our clothes from last night, still on the floor in front of the couch where we left them in our haste. None of his clothes are left in the bedroom closet here, so he'll have to make his way into the living room to get dressed in the open. I've never felt so awkward around him in all the years I've known him. This isn't natural at all.

But why I walked to the kitchen wrapped in my sheet instead of grabbing my robe from the bathroom is beyond me. Walking back into the bedroom now isn't possible. He's lying in my bed... naked. I'll hide in the kitchen, then when he joins me for coffee, he'll be fully dressed and I'll be in a sheet, toga-style.

This is the worst walk of shame in the history of hookups... and it's in my own damn kitchen and with my own damn husband.

"Liv, should I go? Do you want me to leave?"

He speaks from directly behind me, when I'm making sure I added more coffee before leaving last night. I didn't hear him walk up, and his question startles me, making me jump and turn toward him at the same time. I try to hide how much the words hurt, but I'm caught off guard.

How do I answer that question? It's much more complicated than the simplistic way he asked. There are numerous meanings behind the words, and I'm not sure even he knows exactly which one he's asking.

Should he leave because we're in the middle of a divorce and he thinks last night was a mistake?

Is he asking because he knows there's no hope of salvaging what we had?

Or is he feeling insecure and doesn't know if I want him here?

He's leaning against the doorjamb, barefoot, shirtless, and wearing his jeans unbuttoned. He has sexy bed hair, and I'm sure mine looks more like a twisted mess of a bird's nest. It's unfair of him to look so good first thing in the morning.

"What do you want, Ryder?" I decide to return his vague, multiple-entendre question back to him. Maybe his answer will reveal the true intention behind his question.

"I want..." He pauses, his brow furrowed and his hand scraping across his chin while he's deep in thought. Then he raises his eyes back to mine. "I want exactly what I've always wanted, Liv."

I nod, despite the invisible arrow that pierced my heart. "Then you already have your answer and know what you should do. Since what you want has *always* been the same, why did you even bother with bringing me home last night and staying? You should've just walked away and left me alone, Ryder. Sign the papers and give me full custody of Kiwi."

"Why the hell would I do that?"

"Because our life together was never good enough for you. There's a great big world out there just waiting for Ryder King to show up at the right place and the right time so it can shower him with gifts from the gods. There's nothing here you want, and that includes Kiwi and me.

"When we got her, you knew it was a lifelong commitment. You know you can't travel the world with her. She needs a home with stability, with someone who loves her and wants to be with her. Not someone who just wants to drop in for a weekend once in a while because he has nowhere better to be. Go. Travel everywhere. Fly. Cruise. Walk. Whatever you have to do, but you're not taking Kiwi with you. That would kill her. If you'd ever had any love for her at all, we wouldn't still be fighting over this. If you really loved her, you'd *want* to do what's best for her."

"Best for *her*? Or best for *you*? Who are we really talking about here, Liv?"

"I'm not the one who's leaving. You know exactly who we're talking about, Ryder."

"To answer your other question, you *asked* me to bring you home last night."

"Yeah, I did. I asked for a ride home, and you chose to spend the night in my bed. Don't you think you've hurt me enough as it is? Seven months of dragging this divorce out just so you can have your way. You're being selfish and stubborn—and those aren't positive traits. You've already broken up our home. Are you trying to break my spirit completely too?"

His jaw drops open and he stammers for an answer. "No. Of course not. I don't want that."

"Then why do you want this custody arrangement? You're leaving, Ryder. How can you leave *and* have custody of Kiwi at the same time? Explain this to me, once and for all, because you haven't been able to articulate it during our mediation sessions." I clutch the sheet tightly in my fist until my fingers ache.

I'm exhausted from wearing my heart on my sleeve for so long, and I simply can't do this anymore. One way or another, this has to end soon.

"I love her too, Liv. You're not the only one who loves her." His voice is softer, but he still hasn't explained his rationale.

"You didn't answer my question. Tell me how this works."

Kiwi lands on my shoulder, and Ryder stares at her for a long minute in silence.

"I love her. I can't simply let her go. Even if I don't know what to do with it, she's part of me now."

Our pet bird is, but *I'm* not. He doesn't say the words out loud, but then he doesn't have to. What he didn't say speaks loudly enough on its own.

"Here's the answer to your question, Ryder. Yes, you should leave. Right now. And don't ever come back. You can pick Kiwi up at the shop when it's time. But don't ever come back to *my* house again."

I move to the front door, twist the deadbolt, and open the door wide. His cue to leave couldn't be any clearer, so he picks up his shirt, socks, and shoes and walks out of what used to be *our* house for the last time.

My heart and my mind are finally on the same page. This is now my house, and there are no remnants of us left to salvage. If he doesn't sign the papers by

Monday's mediation session, I will. It'll kill me to see him take her on one of his big adventure trips because I know how miserable and sick she'll be. I can only hope he changes his mind when the time comes for his journey.

Without watching him drive away, I close and lock the door. Then I make Kiwi's breakfast and put her back in her room while I shower. The water washes away the traces of last night, taking the last of my tears with it. I'm taking today to grieve and wallow in my self-pity, then tomorrow I'm moving on with my life. I'm legally separated. The dissolution of my marriage has been underway long enough, and everyone in this town is fully aware of all the drama we've created.

After I dry off, I grab my sketchbook from my car and curl up on the couch. Kiwi joins me as I pour my feelings onto the blank pages, creating works of art that somehow give me a renewed sense of purpose and direction. This part of my life is all mine. I haven't shared it with anyone, not even Ryder, when we were still close. I don't plan on telling anyone about it anytime soon. Inviting others to critique and assess this part of my mind feels way too personal, as if I'm letting the world read my diary.

Perhaps this is my version of a diary because the art I create is wholly dependent on my frame of mind. Today, I'm heartbroken, mad, and distraught, and it shows in my sketches. Flipping through the other pages, I see a distinct difference on the days when I was happy or playful.

A picture is worth a thousand feelings.

When the phone rings, I glance at the time and realize I've been sketching new designs for hours. I pick up my cell and see Faith's smiling face on the screen and decide to take it. If I don't, she'll just show up here to check on me, and I'm not in any shape to have company today.

"Hey." My abrupt greeting is a dead giveaway.

"That bad, huh? Tell me everything and don't leave anything out."

She's silent while I fill her in on the events of the night after she left Pony Up early and as I describe the shitshow of a morning I had.

"You had sex with him while going through a divorce? Is that what you just told me? Are you serious?"

"Yes, that's what I just told you, and I am serious. I'm also serious when I say it's over. *Over* over. If he doesn't sign the papers and agree to my demands on Monday, I'll sign and agree to his. Then we can go before the judge and finalize our divorce once and for all." I throw my pencil down and watch it bounce across the coffee table.

"Liv, you're both making a monumental mistake. How do neither of you see what's happening?"

"I do see it, Faith. I believe he loved me at one time, but obviously it wasn't enough for him to make his home here with me. The life we've built together doesn't satisfy him. He wants something different from what I can give. How much clearer can it be?"

"Liv, I say this with all the love in my heart. You are every bit as stubborn as Ryder and you won't listen to reason either. You have to learn everything the hard way. I'm afraid you're about to learn quite a bit."

"Thanks for the pep talk, my bestie. I'm going to go turn on the gas oven and dry my hair now. Talk to you tomorrow?"

"Of course. Don't leave your head in the oven too long though. It may bake some sense into you. Call me if you need me. Love you."

"Thank you. Love you."

CHAPTER 6

Ryder

It's Monday morning and I'm sitting in Java Jitters, waiting for my morning coffee, when Hattie and Hazel Jackson approach my table. For the record, being their target is never a good thing. They're sisters who probably mean well at the heart of things, but they're known as the town gossips. Hattie, with her blue hair and customary plaid shirt, along with Hazel, with her Sunday best and bright red lipstick on, are too much to take on a good day.

This morning is not a good day.

"Well, well, well, look who it is, Hazel." Hattie smirks at me with a shit-eating grin. The rest of the morning patrons turn to listen because everyone knows what's coming next.

"Oh, I see him, Hattie. We know all about this one, don't we?"

"We sure do." Hattie's smirk increases. They're trying to bait me so they can close in for the kill. I'm not biting. "We have the scoop on him."

"Good morning, ladies. It's nice to see you both looking so chipper this morning. I'm just waiting for Jessie to finish with my breakfast order before I start my day."

"That jolt of coffee gives you plenty of energy, doesn't it?" Hattie's smirk turns into a full smile. It's a little scary.

"Yeah, I guess it does."

"Did you have a good weekend, Ryder?" Hazel asks, somewhat pointedly.

Fucking hell.

The MC Scoop.

Someone kill me now. I know exactly what they're talking about, except I don't know what details were shared.

Tate Michaels must have written a piece about me on her blog. That gossip column is like crack for the people of Mason Creek. Tate has a way of finding out private information about everyone and sharing it on her blog, mostly before it's ready for public consumption.

"It was fair." I shrug, trying to dismiss their attempts to poke more into my personal life.

"The way I read it, you had more than a fair weekend. Seems it was a downright *scream*." Hattie tries to get her jab in without laughing in my face. She tries but fails.

"You shouldn't believe everything you read, Hattie. You know how people like to spread rumors and talk about things they didn't witness firsthand." All eyes are on me, but their smiles hide behind their coffee cups.

"Maybe I prefer to believe this story, Ryder." Hattie shrugs and lays a piece of paper on the table in front of me. "I printed it out for you, in case you want to frame it or something."

Hattie and Hazel retreat to their table, the one they claim to have reserved for every morning so no one else can take their spot. They leave me alone, but still watch my every move with their penetrating eyes. With all the strength I can muster, I pick up the article and start reading, knowing I'll regret this decision with every single word.

Hear ye! Hear ye!

I've always wanted an occasion to use that phrase, but none of the previous Scoops quite fit the bill to earn that distinction.

Until now.

And I can't wait to share the details of why this phrase is so perfectly fitting for today's Scoop.

If you were anywhere in the vicinity of the home formerly shared by the soon-to-be-exes, Mr. and Mrs. Ryder King, you probably heard all the screams and howls that lasted well into the wee hours of the morning. To the untrained ear and the unknowing resident, you'd swear the noises came from a female fox in heat, screaming for her mate to perform his natural duties. And who could blame you for assuming that was the case? Certainly not this Scooper, considering the decibel levels were so similar.

But that's not the case AT ALL, my dear reader.

No.

But keep reading because you'll want to know every sordid detail of this Scoop!

Friday night's earsplitting and animated escapades were not scenes from the Discovery Channel or Animal Planet, although I'm considering contacting both channels to have our little town showcased in their documentaries... starring none other than Ryder and Olivia King.

Yes, folks, all those noises were from the rowdy and raucous relations from two of our favorite Mason Creek citizens.

The perfect couple, who separated seven months ago, have been involved in intense negotiations with our local mediator in numerous attempts to finalize their divorce. This journalist must ask: Are Mr. and Mrs. King reconciling now, or was this a case of too much alcohol and a lack of other options in Small Town, USA?

Only time will tell.

Keep your eyes open, your ears to the ground, and my email address on speed send, Scoopers. We'll get to the bottom of this episode of Ex Marks the Spot together! For those of you who were within earshot of the house in question, I highly recommend getting a hearing test now, just to be on the safe side.

Oh. My. God.

How...

Who...

Where...

I have so many questions I can't bring myself to formulate fully because I don't know if having the answers will make this situation better or worse. All I know right now is I'm still the sole focus of everyone in the café, including all the new people who walked in while I was reading the recount of my very private night with Liv. I'm doing my best to maintain my composure and not verbally assault everyone in here.

"Your breakfast is getting cold," Jessie yells out to everyone and no one in particular. "Eat up, people. There's nothing to see here."

She stops at my table with my order in a to-go bag. I didn't order it that way, but I'm grateful for her big heart and ability to read the room.

"Thanks, Jessie."

"Ryder, I know it's easier said than done, but don't let this bullshit get you down. People around here clearly need more work to do to keep them busy and out of everyone else's business. Walk out with your head held high and take care of your situation. You have nothing to be ashamed of because you've done nothing wrong. What happens between a man and woman in their own home isn't anyone else's concern."

"You're absolutely right, Jessie. Thanks for the pep talk." I carry my breakfast bag and coffee in one hand and grab the printed article off the table with the other. "This is going in the garbage, where it belongs."

No one makes eye contact with me as I stroll to the door, paper in hand. My demeanor leaves no room for doubt—I'm not fucking around with this nonsense today. Creating an article about what happened between my wife and me in our bed crossed the line. Most would say that's typical of Tate, since she loves to gossip and share every shred of information she receives. But being on the receiving end of that attention doesn't feel very good.

To be fair, my mood was shit before this article was laid in my lap. My last conversation with Livvy made me question everything I thought I knew and wanted. When she pinned me with the logical question of how I planned to have this grand, adventurous life while dragging Kiwi from place to place, I honestly didn't have an answer. Not one I could give her anyway.

But when I envisioned that life without Liv in it, I couldn't breathe or think. The last several months have been pure hell, no doubt, but deep down I always thought she'd relent and join me. When the ugly truth smacked me in the face and I realized I'd truly lost my wife, nothing else in my life made sense. Not one single part of it means anything without her by my side.

What good is any accomplishment I achieve if Liv's not there to share it with me?

When I walked out of my lonely condo this morning, I'd decided to stop the mediation attempts and ask Liv to give us another chance. My deepest darkest is still securely secret, but I'm racking my brain to find a way around it. Now that the extremely personal and inappropriate article about us has hit the internet, I'm afraid she'll be so pissed she won't hear me out. There's no way she hasn't already heard about it. But I hurry to George's office as fast as I can go, anyway.

I have to mitigate the damage as soon as possible.

Liv's already seated in the small conference room when I walk in. My entry catches her attention, but she barely shifts her gaze toward me.

"Liv, can we talk?" I purposely keep my voice low and nonconfrontational. I'm upset about the invasion into our love life too, but we can get past this.

"There's nothing left to talk about. I've signed the papers. George took them to Judge Nelson to get his final signature. Since we've had the legal separation in place for at least six months, our marriage will be dissolved as soon as his signature dries on the paper." Then she turns her icy gaze to me. "Congratulations, Ryder. You'll be free to move away from here in a matter of minutes now."

"What? No, Liv. Wait. Just wait. Where is George

now?" Panic rises in my chest. The anxiety threatens to overtake me. Our marriage is over? With a stroke of a pen?

"Wait? Wait for what? You've had long enough to change your mind. It's too late now. It's over, Ryder. There's no going back." She folds her arms across her body, closing herself off from me and ending any chance to talk more about it.

"Well, not so fast, young lady." Judge Nelson enters the room with a stack of papers in his hand. "I have a few questions to ask before I can approve the agreement you signed."

"Ask away. Let's get this over with as quickly as possible. We've wasted enough of everyone's time as it is." She squares her shoulders and sets her jaw. My heart shatters into a bazillion pieces.

He slides a single sheet of paper out of the stack to the middle of the table to let everyone see it. I close my eyes and drop my head because I've already seen it and memorized every word of it.

"Care to explain this to me?" His no-nonsense tone is firmly intact.

"What is it? I don't know what you're referring to, Judge." Liv reaches across the table as I open my eyes. My knee-jerk reaction is the grab her arm and still her movements. She cuts her eyes over to me, keeping her brows drawn, and cocks her head to the side. "What are you doing, Ryder? Let go."

"Take a deep breath first, Liv. Trust me on this one." She stares me down until I release her arm. In my defense, I'm only trying to help her cope with the violation she's about to experience.

She reads the passage quickly at first, and her bottom jaw drops open. Then she starts over from the top, taking more time to read and absorb every word and not-so-subtle insinuation. The fiery red tinge starts at the base of her neck and works its way across her face, disappearing into her hairline.

"What in the actual fuu—"

"Olivia, I understand it's upsetting, but I'll warn you now to watch your language in here. This may be an informal setting, but this is still a formal meeting."

"Yes, sir." She barely gets the words past her gritted teeth. "How can she write this about us and get away with it?"

"Then it's true? You two spent the night together and had intercourse?" His attention darts back and forth between Liv and me, waiting for us to confirm or deny the gossip that's clearly gripped our small town. "Don't even think about lying to me."

Naturally we were thinking about lying to him. Does he think we're stupid? The judge doesn't make an appearance during our mediation sessions for nothing. His presence here signals a significant shift in the paradigm.

We're both still silent. It's awkward and uncomfortable. He asked if we had sex as easily as if he'd asked about the weather instead. Liv's sunburnt-red skin hasn't lessened at all, and I don't think she has the ability to speak.

"It's true, Judge. As humiliating and mortifying as that article is, I drove Liv home from Pony Up and spent the rest of the night with her. We didn't think it was anyone else's business, but obviously the cat's out of the bag." I try to spare Liv of the lascivious details Tate had fun recounting in her column by glossing over them in my retelling to the judge.

"You're right, Ryder, it's no one else's business. However, I'm afraid it is *my* business. You see, having intercourse during the mediation process before the divorce is final constitutes a reconciliation. If you're still set on proceeding with the divorce, I'll give you two options. One, you can start the six-month separation period over again, abstaining from having sex the entire time, and I'll sign the agreement. Or you can go to marriage counseling. After sufficient time has passed for the therapist to get to know you and analyze your relationship, if she agrees the irreconcilable differences claim still stands, I'll make an exception and finalize it at that time. Which option will it be?"

"How long is 'sufficient time' for her to get to know us?" Liv challenges, her voice rising slightly with each word. She pinches her lips together, probably to avoid saying something to the judge she'll regret later.

"That's up to the therapist. I'm not putting a time limit on it. If she can give a definitive answer after a few weeks, I'll accept her expert opinion. Do you have a problem with my decision? I think I'm being overly understanding, considering the circumstances since this began."

"No, I think you're being fair. It's just that... I *finally* signed the papers today and I thought I could put this behind me. This whole ordeal has been an intense drain on my emotions, and this is just the icing on the cake." She drops her head into her hands, shielding her face from everyone as she works through her feelings.

"I understand, but your recent actions have tied my hands, legally speaking. Because of that, I need an answer from both of you before you leave here today." Judge Nelson waits for our reply with an expressionless stare.

My heart urges me to pick the six months option, giving me more time to convince her this isn't the best path for us after all. But now I see the toll this drawn-out fight is taking on her well-being. She is weary after the constant clashes and being torn in different directions. My head realizes the right thing to do is let the therapist make the decision.

Letting her go is the least painful option for her. I can't keep hurting her like this, even though losing her is killing me.

"We'll go to the marriage counseling sessions. I'll participate in whatever she tells us to do." I turn my attention to Liv. With raised eyebrows, I silently ask if she agrees.

"Fine. Let's do it. What happens if the therapist doesn't recommend a divorce?"

Judge Nelson shrugs. "You start the six-month separation period over again. I can't force you to stay married, only to follow the letter of the law."

"Great. Marriage counseling should be a blast. Can't wait." Liv rolls her eyes as she stands to leave.

She doesn't catch it as she storms out of the conference room, but I can't miss the smirk on the judge's face.

CHAPTER 7

Olivia

I'm so grateful to have two employees who can run my business when I need time for myself. Annie and Jasmine have been lifesavers over the last couple of weeks while I've worked through a tsunami of emotions. Some days, I felt like I was hanging ten on the biggest wave in the ocean, making it my personal bitch. Other days, I've questioned how I've managed a successful business when I seem to have the emotional control of a small toddler.

Too bad today's time away from my shop is to start the marriage counseling sessions. I'm dreading it more than I've told anyone. It's been two weeks since Judge Nelson asked us to make an impossible choice. If I have to go through another six months of this limbo purgatory, I'll need therapy for a very different reason.

Most days, I feel as though I'll drown from the crushing weight of what's become my new life. The days I spend alone at home because Kiwi is with Ryder are some of the loneliest hours I've ever experienced. Though I know there's nothing Faith wouldn't do to help me, she has her own life to live. She can't babysit me through my mental breakdown, take care of her daughter, and stoke the fires of her own love life all at the same time.

So, I've weathered these days on my own... and that forced me to take a long, hard look in the mirror. I didn't like everything I saw, and recognizing my own faults and failures added to my depression at first. Then I realized something that helped me straighten my crown and stand tall again. There's strength in being able to admit when I'm wrong. I've taken small steps to better understand myself and what makes me tick. Moving forward is better than standing still.

Today is Ryder's day to take Kiwi for his week. Shared custody of our pretty girl only gets harder the longer we do it. Instead of coming to my house, he now picks her up at work and takes her to the jewelry store with him. He's respected my demand for him to stay away from the home we used to share. Ryder keeping his distance from me should make this process easier.

But it doesn't.

For some, "out of sight, out of mind" is absolutely true. But for me, "absence makes the heart grow fonder" seems more fitting.

Seeing him only reminds me of what I've lost and will never have again.

Because I'm all too aware of how morose I sound, I keep my thoughts to myself. Any hint of what's really on my mind and those around me feel as if they have to console me. That's not what I want or need, but I realize they're only trying to help. I've heard every variation of "you're still young, you'll find someone else" there is.

The only way that would happen is if I left this town. Everything here reminds me of Ryder. The places we used to go together, the things we used to do, and the good times we've had. All our firsts happened right here, and it seems all our lasts will too. Since I'm not interested in moving away, my chances of remarrying are slim to none. Besides, I know most every man who's remotely close to my age. They're more like brothers than anything else, and that thought is just not appealing.

Thinking about the devil apparently conjures him.

"Hi, Livvy. How are you?" Ryder stops in front of me, looking uncomfortable as the only man in a store full of revealing lingerie.

"Fine. You?" It's a rhetorical question. I'm not asking him to update me on his life since I last saw him. I've found keeping our conversations to a minimum is best for my mental health. It also slows down the wagging tongues and active fingers of the town's grapevine.

"Honestly, it's been a tough week." He waits for me to engage and ask for details, but I can't be drawn into him again.

"This beautiful girl will keep you company and make you forget about your week." I hold out my hand and Kiwi hops on it.

"Oh, you found some new designs to carry. I don't remember seeing these in the store inventory before now." He examines the garment rack containing the new pieces. "Why is there only one of each?"

"Because each one is so unique and different from my usual catalog. I'm testing these to determine the top two most requested. It doesn't make sense to have a half dozen of each on hand if they like only one or two of them. If no one likes them, I'm only out the money these six designs cost."

"That's smart. You know, maybe you should have a runway show in here so the women can see them on a real body. You'd probably get a ton of orders that night." He smiles warmly, taking me aback. He's never been interested in my lingerie store before. I mean, he always asked about my day, and we talked about business topics often, but this detailed suggestion is over-the-top for Ryder.

"What a great idea, Ry. I could call it 'Draw the Shades' night and send invitations to my customers. Word of mouth pulls more people in than anything. The fear of missing out is a real motivator."

"It sure is, so use it to your advantage. Whisper about it around town and it'll appear in Tate's column before you can blink. *The MC Scoop* will scoop this up. It's salacious and forbidden, and those are two qualities Tate can't refuse."

"You've kept this marketing genius hidden from me all these years. What else are you hiding?" My foul mood momentarily lifts, and I forget we're going to a therapist this evening so she can eventually tell the judge we don't belong together.

Then the truth slams back into me like a freight train.

"You know that I've never been able to hide anything from you, Livvy. I'm an open book for you to read at any time. You're the one who's always been able to keep surprises from me." His smile remains, but his eyes soften.

This is why I don't talk to him. I know what his expressions mean without him having to tell me what's on his mind. He's reminiscing, allowing our memories to run rampant in his mind and cloud his judgment. Being lonely and having a bad week make him think twice about our current path.

Believe me, I've run this course at least a dozen times a day, but I always hit the same dead end. There's no way around it and we can't go through it.

I don't say it out loud, but there was one surprise he was able to hide from me all these years. My non-poker face response must remind him of that fact because he quickly looks away.

"Well, I guess you're here for Kiwi, unless you've developed a new fetish and want to try on some silky lingerie." I pass her to his outstretched hand. "Hang on, let me grab her toys and snacks I made for today before you go."

When I return from the back room, he's nuzzling Kiwi and has his eyes closed. He's always been so affectionate, and maybe that's why I assumed we were on the same page with our lives. Dating, marriage, white picket fence home, lots of babies, and huge family functions—life would be complete. All the things I never had while I was growing up but desperately wanted.

"Here you are." I pass Kiwi's bowl of carrots, corn, sweet potatoes, and peas along with her bag of favorite toys to his free hand.

"Thanks for making her snacks today. I'm picking up groceries after work, so this is a tremendous help."

"It's no problem." She's worth all the trouble in the world.

He dawdles for a moment, shifting from one foot to the other, before finally releasing a heavy sigh. "Well, I should go before you make me model this purple thingamajig around the store as an advertisement for your 'Draw the Shades' night. I'll see you later... this afternoon."

He just remembered our appointment.

Naked Eyes got it right when they sang "Always Something There to Remind Me."

"Yeah. I'll see you later." I watch him walking away until he's out of sight.

When I return to the counter to start planning the runway event, something else he said sparks an idea. Until now, my focus has always been on women's lingerie and our specific needs. But now my mind is racing with new ideas, possibly far too innovative and progressive for our sleepy little town. But that's what online shopping is for, and my website gets a fair number of hits.

My secret, the one nobody else knows, is I personally conceived and designed every piece of lingerie I carry in my store. The label isn't under my real name, though sometimes I wish I was brave enough to put it out in front of the world. Then maybe one day, I could join the ranks of Coco Chanel, Donna Karan, and Donatella Versace. A girl can dream. Some days, a hope and a dream are all I have.

This idea started as a project I was assigned in one of my college classes. I dual-majored in business and fashion merchandising and design, and I had to build a fashion brand and turn it into a profitable business for one of my classes. I already had a knack for sketching, but I'd never thought about turning that ability into a profitable business. The research I had to do to pass the class inspired me to put pencil to paper, so to speak. My notebooks full of fashion ideas turned into a lucrative side hustle when I contacted a manufacturer with my specifications.

My sorority sisters kept me in business with new requests and suggestions for new pieces every week. Then they started sharing my creations with their friends and family members, and my business really took off. The funny thing was, I anonymously posted an order form on our house online bulletin board. My online payment account was under a business name, so no one ever connected the dots pointing to me. No one ever knew I was the one behind the designs.

When Ryder and I moved back to Mason Creek, I kept that part of my business to myself. Not because I felt ashamed of anything, but because I liked keeping the creative part of my process to myself. Designing something beautiful and sexy and innovative with the world is akin to reading my diary over the loudspeaker to the entire high school. After keeping my secret for so long, I found it easier not to talk about it than to confess to my covert activities.

Every day, I sketch new designs at work during normal hours and email the specs to my contact at the manufacturer before I leave the back office. Over the years I've been doing this, I've built a considerable catalog of naughty wear, designed to make all women feel beautiful, sexy, and desirable.

Now I'm going to do the same for the men. They all may not wear the pieces I've created for the ladies, but plenty of men want to feel desired and appreciated. They'll go the extra mile for their significant others.

Something unexpected happened during my two weeks of solo soul searching. At first, I was torn about celebrating it because the rest of my life is going up in flames. But a sense of pride and validation swells in my chest every time I think about it. The editor-in-chief, Jaqueline Rafferty, for the high-end fashion magazine *Entranced* contacted me about my lingerie line.

One of the magazine's employee came across some of my pieces online. She was blown away by the design and searched for my label. After she perused the catalog on my website, she immediately called Jaqueline so they could view it together. Now, they want to feature my label in an upcoming issue to help spread the word about my products.

In my wildest dreams, I never imagined Queen's Unmentionables would take me in this direction. Of course, I immediately agreed to a full five-page spread in a magazine that charges nearly $200,000 for a single-page advertisement. The print and online version have over thirty-two million combined subscribers. Just the thought of that many people seeing my creations makes me nauseous and elated at the same time. I figure the worst that can happen is I have a couple of months with high traffic on my website before everyone loses interest and moves on to the next hot topic.

But for those few weeks, I'll enjoy the limelight, even if it is under my pseudonym.

My hand flies across the sketch pad, creating one drawing after the other of designer undergarments for men. After my seventeenth design, I force myself to stop and scan them into my computer so the manufacturer can make and ship the sample sizes with rush delivery. If I'm drawing the shades at the shop, I might as well add a few men to the mix and spice it up.

Maybe then they won't be so embarrassed to step

foot in here. I mail so many local packages it's pathetic. Man-up and walk in here already.

"Liv? Livvy? Earth to Olivia. Are you in there?"

I glance up and find Jasmine waving her hand in front of my face, trying to get my attention. "Oh, sorry, sweetie. It's hard to break my concentration when I'm on a roll. What can I do for you?"

"It's time for your therapy session. You don't want to be late your first day." She gives me a small smile, but only because I didn't tell her about the appointment.

The entire town already knows my schedule.

Maybe one of them can tell me when I'm supposed to check into the mental hospital. I could really use a break from reality for a little while.

"Thanks, Jasmine. You're right, I need to run. Are you okay to lock up by yourself tonight?"

"Sure. I got this. Don't worry about a thing." She puts her hand on my shoulder in a show of solidarity, as if the next hour will be so traumatizing, I can't recover.

I force a smile I don't feel, pushing aside the frustration of being gossiped about by the entire town since the day my parents moved here. "All right, I'll see you tomorrow, then. Have a good evening."

After stuffing my sketchbook and pencils in my bag, I grab my phone from the counter and rush out before Jasmine starts crying on my behalf. Maybe it's only in my mind after the *MC Scoop* article, but I'd swear that everyone I meet on the way to Dr. Carlson's office watches me with the same sad face Jasmine gave me. It's only a block away, but I think I've encountered every citizen of Mason Creek in that short distance.

Allie McDougal, our local therapist, occupies a room in the doctor's office a couple days a week and sees people at her home in the next town over from here on the other days. She's not from Mason Creek, which makes this whole business of talking about the intimate details of my life much easier. If she'd been someone I'd gone to school with, I would've chosen the six-month option instead and exiled myself to Glacier National Park until it was over.

When I rush through the door to her office, Ryder has already made himself comfortable on the couch and has Allie laughing over his mischief. The ethical code of conduct requirement between a doctor and patient flashes in my mind, but I push it aside. Or try to, anyway. Never mind how pretty she is, or the way she's perfectly manicured from head to toe, or that she's genuinely a nice person. Seeing the two of them in a remotely flirty situation sets my teeth on edge.

This will be a long hour.

CHAPTER 8

Ryder

Our four o'clock appointment has been on my mind all day. I had to force myself to think of anything else. Focusing on my work is like asking a four-year-old child to walk through Willy Wonka's chocolate factory without touching anything.

It's absolutely impossible.

Unable to stand around talking about jewelry any longer, I leave my store in the capable hands of my assistant manager, Marcus. Kiwi and I take a leisurely stroll down Baylor Street, which is in the complete opposite direction from Dr. Carlson's office. Stopping at the corner of West Old Bridge Road, I stare at the covered bridge entrance to our tiny town.

It's also the way out.

If I put that old bridge in my rearview mirror, I'll leave behind everything that has ever meant anything to me. If I don't, I'm afraid I'll become one of those old men around town. The ones who sit on the park benches and watch everyone else live their lives. They're living statues, and everyone knows all about their personal business.

I want more than that.

Then again, Liv is all I want.

At least I'm not indecisive.

Around the corner and past the barber shop, I pass Java Jitters and see Jessie. She's busy as usual behind the display case. My feet know where I'm going if my brain hasn't informed me of a conscious decision yet. One more turn onto the town square, and I'm back in front of Queen's Unmentionables.

Like most of our town, I thought Liv was joking when she said she was opening a lingerie store. Here. In Mason Creek. Across from the mayor's office. Right on the town square so everyone can see her panties, thongs, and more.

When I realized she was serious, I was mortified inside. The ridicule we'd get from everyone else would be unbearable, I was sure of it. Of course, there were some who were vehemently opposed to having such private clothing articles on display in a prominent location, but the majority of the town surprised me.

They fully supported her venture and frequented her store.

Liv chose the name of the business solely to spite those who opposed her livelihood. Queen's Unmentionables was born to shame those who were ashamed of her. Queen, for obvious reasons. She's my queen and I'm her King, pun intended. Unmentionables, to make them see it every single day.

She has a little bit of a mean streak.

Kiwi and I sit on a bench across from the lingerie store, waiting for Liv to come out before we head to the doctor's office for our appointment. If we happen to bump into each other on the sidewalk, there's no reason why we can't walk together.

"Momma? Momma?" Kiwi asks and turns her head as she looks at me.

"Yeah, baby, Momma's coming."

"So sexy." Then she lets out a loud catcall whistle.

"Where did you learn that?" I wait for her to answer, as if she understands my question.

Then I look back at Liv's shop and see her through the front picture window. She's behind the counter, but she's furiously working on something with her hands. Whatever she's doing, it has her full attention. Maybe she's planning the "Draw the Shades" night we talked about earlier today.

She was surprised by my suggestion for a good

reason. I've never been as supportive of her business as I should've been. All it took was losing my one true love to make me realize all the places I've fallen short as her husband and partner in life. No one else's opinion should've mattered to me. I shouldn't have cared about what the town ninnies said or thought. All Liv needed was my encouragement and support.

Now look at her.

She's flourished even without my help. Maybe even in spite of me. Have I been any better than those who persecuted her? Maybe I didn't actively oppose it, but my passive stance didn't help either. The marketing suggestion I made earlier was simply one small attempt to start making up for my past mistakes.

My watch vibrates from the fifteen-minute alarm I set as a reminder. When it's clear Liv won't be out in the next couple of minutes, I decide to walk to the office alone. I'll still get there early, but I can take care of all the paperwork so Liv doesn't have to spend time doing it when she arrives. Meeting our therapist alone for a few minutes first may not be such a bad idea either.

Allie calls me back to her comfortable and inviting office almost as soon as I arrive. With the court mandate in place, she already has most of the information she needs on us.

"What a pretty bird. Can I hold her? Will she bite?" Allie's attention is solely focused on Kiwi.

"Sure, you can hold her. Just let her perch on your hand. She may use her beak to climb on you, but she's not doing it out of aggression. No reason to be afraid."

Allie holds her hand up to Kiwi's breast and Kiwi steps on to it. As expected, she walks up Allie's arm, grabs her sleeve with her beak, and hops up to Allie's shoulder.

"Hello." Kiwi turns her head from side to side, examining Allie.

"Hello, there. Aren't you a pretty girl?"

"Yes," Kiwi replies.

Allie chuckles as Kiwi flies back to my shoulder. "Snack, Daddy."

I pull the small plastic bag with her leftovers out of my pocket and feed her a carrot slice. Then I sit on the couch and wait for Liv to arrive.

"Are you not afraid she'll fly away from you?"

"No, her wings are clipped so she can't fly fully. She can flap her wings to glide a few feet. But we're her family, so she wouldn't go far, anyway. These birds need nearly constant companionship."

"She's amazing. I wish my pets could talk to me. Now you have to bring her with you to every session." We both laugh, then I look over and see Liv rushing in at the last minute.

"Well, we don't leave her alone for long periods of time, so I'm sure you'll see her frequently."

"Momma. Momma." Kiwi bobs up and down, excited to see Liv again. Liv sits on the couch beside me so Kiwi can be close to both of us. This is how we always sat at home too—when we still lived together. The constant close proximity helped Kiwi bond with us equally.

Liv leans over and nuzzles her cheek against Kiwi's. She's so close to me, and her perfume brings back so many memories. All I want to do is gather her in my arms and make this all go away. I'm just not sure how we can get back to where we once were again. There are too many reasons why we shouldn't be together. But I'm willing to try if I can convince her our reunion is best for all of us. Hopefully our therapist will see it and help guide us back together.

"Sorry I'm a little late. I got busy at work and completely lost track of time." Liv continues to scratch the side of Kiwi's head when she speaks to Allie.

"No problem at all. Kiwi stole the show as soon as she entered the room. She's fascinating. No wonder you both love her so much." Allie obviously already caught up on the major points of our case. Her polite but professional tone indicates the session officially has started now. "So, let's start from the beginning. What brings you two here today?"

Talk about a loaded question. Where do I even start to answer that? I could tell her I'm still in love with my wife and can't see my future without her in it. Or I could point out how Liv asked me to take her home from the bar and we fell back in bed together as if it was the most natural act in the world. That definitely points to a reconciliation, even though we claim to be irreconcilable. Or maybe I should lead with...

"Ryder and I want the complete opposite things in life. Whether we still love each other is irrelevant if one of us is forced to forfeit our hopes and dreams so the other can have theirs. That only leads to resentment down the road. We can't be husband and wife anymore, but I certainly don't want anything to happen that would make us end up hating each other. Making a clean break now is the best option." Liv folds her hands on her lap, keeps her back straight as a board, and her tone even throughout her little speech.

She so rehearsed that little speech ahead of time.

"Ryder, what is your answer to why you're here today?" Allie's deadpan expression gives nothing away.

"Liv and I have grown apart and have very different expectations regarding the next phase of our lives. It's something we failed to discuss fully and agree upon the timelines and specifics before we married. We were too young and blinded by love to think anything could come between us." My answer is the truth, but I'm careful not to convey the wrong message. I don't believe we're beyond fixing.

Allie makes notes in her journal but doesn't respond otherwise to either of our explanations. "How old were you when you married?"

"Twenty-two," Liv replies. "Ryder proposed during our junior year of college, and we married soon after graduation."

"How did he propose to you?" Allie looks up from her notes, engaging with Liv on a more personal level.

Liv's facial features soften, and a small smile plays on her lips. I can see from the dreamy expression on her face, her mind is taking her back to that night when the world only revolved around her and me.

"We were home on Christmas break nine years ago. Winter had started out abnormally hard that year. The temperatures were much colder than we usually have. We had more significant snow days than normal, and everything was frozen. The lake was a solid block of ice on the top several feet. Limbs snapped under the weight of the snow in the forest all around Mason Creek. It was just really unusual so early in the season.

"Anyway, Ryder had already made up this big elaborate plan in his mind and Mother Nature was not stopping him. He and I always enjoyed long walks in the woods and exploring new hiking trails, so it wasn't unusual for him to pick me up and say, 'Let's go get lost today.' And that's exactly what he did.

"You can imagine my surprise when he drove into town, parked beside the fire station, and got out of his truck. I mean, it's kind of hard to get lost in downtown Mason Creek. But he opened my door, took my hand in his, and I followed him anyway. The sun had already set, and the snow sparkled in the moonlight as we walked through the woods. When we reached the old bridge built by Henry Davis, the view was surreal. The blizzard conditions had eased to a gentle snowfall. Huge flakes hung in the cold air. The water under the bridge was completely frozen. Stars twinkled in the black skies. An enormous elk with the most beautiful antlers I've ever seen stepped out of the tree line and just basked in the moonlight, unafraid of our presence. When I turned to get Ryder's attention, he was down on one knee with a beautiful ring in his hand."

She stops talking—cold. She's told this story a million times, so I know she's not finished. After a silence long enough to start feeling awkward, I make myself look up from my lap. I've avoided looking at her during the entire story because it's hard enough remembering it in my own mind. Watching her face as she relives it moment by moment is too much.

My heart drops to my stomach and my lungs forget how to function.

Tears stream down her face unchecked, and she bites her lower lip to try to stop it from trembling. I look at Allie for any hint of guidance, but she doesn't return my gaze. Her eyes are locked on Liv's face, assessing every emotion and reaction she's displaying.

After another moment, Liv regains her composure and continues the retelling of our engagement.

"Ryder said he'd loved me from the day I moved to Mason Creek as a child. He knew he'd found his soul mate before he was old enough to know what that word meant. Then he asked me to spend the rest of my life with him and make him the happiest man in the world. He promised to meet my every need and do whatever it took to give me the best life." She sniffles and wipes her face with a tissue from the table beside her. "How could I say no to that?"

"Did you believe he would fulfill those promises?"

Liv considers her question for a minute before answering. "At that moment, of course I did. But that was the romantic young girl in me. No one person can meet your every need or give you a perfect life. Happiness has to come from inside you before anyone else has a chance of making you happy. And no matter what he did or how hard he tried to please me, my happiness is ultimately my responsibility."

"And were you happy being married to Ryder?" Allie probes a little more into Liv's thoughts. "Or have you been unhappy with him for a while and just didn't know how to tell him?"

"Of course I was happy with him. We had a great marriage, and we were building a wonderful life together. Why would you assume I wasn't happy with him?"

"Because you're getting a divorce." Allie makes a valid point. "What happened that took away from your happiness from one day to the next? What made you stop loving Ryder?"

"That's a little unfair, Allie. No one who's madly in love wakes up one day and decides they don't like their spouse and they want a divorce. Those marriages break down over time, and usually not from one big event. More often than not, it's all the little things that add up and create an unhappy atmosphere. Asking Liv to pinpoint one thing and one that made her stop loving me is out of line. It also puts all the blame on one person, and we all know that is rarely ever the case." I lean forward on the couch, pinning Allie with my challenging gaze.

"You're quick to defend the woman who's divorcing you, Ryder. Do you think she'd file to dissolve your marriage if she still loved you?"

"Hold on a minute. I never said I quit loving him. I've also never said our problems were all his fault. What I *did* say was we want such completely different things now, there's no way we can both have it our way. Neither of us should have to feel as though we're giving up a vital need in order to satisfy the other person. How did you turn that statement into insinuating Ryder did something wrong that made me quit loving him?"

Allie places her journal on her desk and looks at us with a warm smile. She just made a complete one-eighty from her demeanor not even three seconds ago.

"Thank you for your honesty. Here's what I want to point out. You two are both being so polite and mature about this. But we all know relationships are messy. There are ups and downs, and sometimes those extremes last for a long time. That stands to reason that divorces, in turn, are also messy. You've been in mediation for seven months because you can't come to an agreement, not because everything is perfectly amicable.

"Before I stand in front of the judge and give my honest opinion, I need to see and hear more honesty from both of you. The good, the bad, the ugly—as long as it's the truth, I don't care. But this polite, casual goodbye you're trying to sell me isn't real at all, or you would've already been divorced and moved on with your lives. I hope we all understand each other now."

"Oh, we absolutely understand each other much

better now." Liv doesn't even attempt to hide her hostility from Allie.

"Great." Allie ignores the passive barb and picks up her planner from her desk. "I think meeting once a week for the next several weeks is best. That'll give me a chance to get to know you both better without dragging this out for another seven months. How does Thursday of next week at the same time work for both of you?"

"Fine."

"Great."

Liv and I reply at the same time.

Allie's smile doesn't falter as her eyes dart between us. "It's a date then. Feel free to bring Kiwi back with you anytime."

CHAPTER 9

Olivia

"Can you believe the nerve of that woman?" I throw my hands up in the air, completely frustrated with today's session. "I wonder if we can change therapists."

"That was unprofessional, in my opinion. But she did have a point about us not confronting our problems head-on. She already has our case file, so I don't know if we can change now. Besides, there aren't any other counselors here for us to see." Ryder walks beside me with a stern set to his jaw.

"That's for standing up for me in there. She flipped the switch on me in a split second. I don't know why she decided to attack me all of a sudden. What kind of crazy therapist does that to her clients?"

"You don't have to thank me for standing up for you. Ever. I'll never let anyone mistreat you."

I can't help but notice the leap my heart makes because of his words.

Our fast pace out of the doctor's office led us straight down the street, almost to my store. This is where we'll part. I'll drive to my house just outside the city limits, and Ryder will continue to the next block or so to his condo. After the last hour of reliving a huge part of our history together, my nerves are frayed, and my emotions are all over the board.

"It seems we'll just have to suck it up and get through these next several weeks the best we can. Our lives are in her crazy hands." We stop at my car. An awkward silence lingers between us, and I nervously play with my keys.

"Momma." Kiwi jumps to my shoulder and burrows underneath my hair.

"She misses you when she's with me." Ryder watches as she finds her spot on the back of my neck.

"She asks for you when she's with me too. I'm not the only one she misses." Kiwi finally settles on one spot, using my hair as her bird blanket. "Maybe I should walk to your condo with her. She'll probably feel better when she sees her toys and her cage."

"That's a good idea. I was also thinking maybe you

shouldn't be alone right now. You seem pretty shaken up because of our therapist. Let's face it, you never cry, especially not like that. I thought you might get mad at me for suggesting it though."

"It's okay, Ryder. We're adults, and we have to think about what's best for Kiwi. We have to be able to talk and see each other in the future. For her sake. Maybe I overreacted when I told you never to come back to the house. Being with someone who understands my predicament would be nice right now. No one knows it better than you do."

We turn at the same time and continue walking toward his building. The silence between us feels more comfortable now.

"You know, I've always loved this old covered bridge. After we moved here, every trip my parents dragged me on seemed like it took forever to get back home. But as a little kid, I knew when I saw the bridge, we were almost home and I'd be happy again."

"Everyone was always so jealous of your extravagant vacations. One group of girls would make up these wild tales of all the things you were doing while you were away. It was harmless. They were trying to live vicariously through you without even realizing it." He gives me his reassuring smile, letting me know I shouldn't be concerned.

"It may have been harmless at first. But my parents never realized how their lavish lifestyle caused so much gossip about me all through school. The tales started small, but they grew taller as the years passed. I've stood my ground, taken the high road, and let it roll off my back more times than I can count. That's why I refused to let my haters prevent me from opening my shop. They weren't going to bully or shame me for helping other women here be confident in who they are."

Ryder stops walking and takes a long, hard look at me. Almost as if he's seeing me for the first time. "Livvy, I never knew all the town gossip affected you like that. You've always laughed it off or did more outrageous stuff just to piss them off."

"Of course I did, Ryder. I couldn't let them break me. Can you imagine the hell my life would've been if I'd broken down in front of them? Never let them see you cry or they'll pick your bones dry."

"You made up that saying." He arches one brow at me.

"Yes, I did. It's been my life motto for as long as I can remember. Repeating that over and over got me through high school. Now that I'm older and can make adult decisions, I prefer to tell them to go fuck themselves. It's much more therapeutic. But still, they'll never see me cry."

"Babe, I'm sorry. I feel like such a complete failure because I never realized how much you dealt with these feelings alone. All this time, I should've shielded you better... carried the burden for you. Why didn't you tell me?"

The sincerity in his voice, I can handle. But the pity? Not so much.

"If I'd needed help, I would've asked. But I had it all under control." If I lie to myself enough times, it'll become the truth. Right?

"Clearly, you were completely fine." There's the sarcastic humor I've always loved about Ryder.

When we reach his condo, he invites me in. This is actually the first time I've been in his bachelor pad. The thought of him being with someone else and bringing her here was too much to bear before I saw the interior. Now that I'm here, I'll have more vivid visions of all his bachelor ways.

Yay me.

"Enough of the morose and morbid talk for one day. Man, if every session is this depressing, I don't know why anyone goes at all. How about a beer, a steak, and a big pan of eco-friendly brownies?" Ryder grins from ear to ear.

"You don't mean..."

"Yes, I absolutely do mean. We need a good laugh. What better way than a batch of feel-good chocolaty goodness?" He waggles his eyebrows and waits for an okay from me.

"Let's do it. We haven't had them in years. We deserve it. Mix those brownies first, Martha Stewart. Get our Snoop Dog on." My smile is the first genuine one I've had in the past two weeks, aside from the day the magazine contacted me.

I briefly consider telling Ryder all about my news—all of it. But after the day I've had, I'm not up for more serious discussions. A meal plus a fun dessert sounds like the perfect getaway solution without leaving the comfort of his condo.

Ryder steps out on his back porch to fire up the grill while I untangle Kiwi from the nest she made in my hair. We always leave her cage door open during the day so she can come and go as she pleases, so I leave her to perch on top of her cage to watch us. Then I move into the kitchen to marinate the steaks and pop the potatoes in the microwave.

"Am I stealing this steak from an important guest? We didn't usually keep fresh ones on hand." The words are out of my mouth before I can stop myself.

Kill me now.

I just asked my husband if he has a date.

He tries and fails to hide his amusement. "I have a semi-standing date with Grayson and his girls. I can buy more steaks before their next visit. Don't worry."

"Do you want a salad with this?" We need to change the subject immediately.

"That does sound good, but I don't have the ingredients to make one." His perplexed expression is too cute for words.

"It's okay. I'll run down to the market and grab everything we need. I won't be long. You can make the brownies while I'm out." I slide my hands back and forth, emphasizing my anticipation.

"Don't worry, babe. I'll make sure you're more relaxed than ever tonight. Don't get lost on your way back from the market." He winks playfully before I head toward the door.

The market is on the opposite side of town, so I power walk to my car and drive the rest of the way. It'll be late enough as it is when we finish eating, and I'll need my ride closer to me. Especially if he makes the extra ingredient in our dessert strong. Inside the store, I rush through the aisles to get all the fresh vegetables for our salad. As I'm heading toward the checkout lanes, I try to remember if I saw salad dressing in his refrigerator.

"Better grab some just in case," I say aloud to myself.

Standing in front of the wall of every imaginable dressing flavor, I reach for one when a familiar voice on the next aisle catches my attention. It's not the voice as much as what's she's saying.

"Now that Ryder King is finally available, I think it's time to make my move. That man is fine with a capital F me." Cyndi McNew is one of the biggest gossips and troublemakers in Mason Creek. I've suspected for years she was the one behind most of the rumors about me.

"He's not back on the market yet, Cyn. He's still married to Olivia. From what I hear, he's not ready to let her go, either. You won't tear him away easily." Nikki Harrison, Cyndi's partner in crime, is always waiting in the wings to help stir the shit pot.

"Olivia Anderson-King is an idiot and a stuck-up bitch. She doesn't deserve a good man like Ryder. She has always thought she was better than everyone in Mason Creek. Just because her parents moved here with all their money. It's time I help move this divorce along. Maybe she'll move away and take her tacky lingerie shop with her." Cyndi sounds so smug.

And jealous.

"What do you have in mind?" Nikki's ready to help, regardless of what Cyndi says next.

"We need a dual attack to split up these two permanently. I'll work on seducing Ryder and rub it in Liv's face. Then we also have to start a believable rumor about her hooking up with some random guy.

He can't be from Mason Creek because that would be too easy to disprove."

"You know, I've been taking Photoshop classes. We could alter a few pictures to make it look like she's meeting a guy out of town. Ryder would never stand for that. He'll dump her on her ass."

Today is not the day, ladies.

I drop the bottle of dressing in the basket and round the corner of the aisle. The shocked expressions on their faces are priceless, but I'm determined to push them both over the edge.

"Hello, ladies. How are you tonight?" I'm playing it cool intentionally, not letting on that I heard anything.

"Fine. It's so good to see you, Olivia. It's been way too long. We should have lunch one day next week if you're free." Cyndi is so fake. I can barely stand to look at her.

"Yeah, of course. You know, you should come by the store and let me show you the new inventory. Those crotchless panties and matching camisole you bought from my store last year must be worn out by now. I have a lot of new items that'll suit your activities."

She stammers but can't form a coherent response. Her face turns bright red, and she avoids looking at Nikki. After trash-talking my store, she's mortified to be outed as a customer.

"We're really sorry to hear about your divorce, Liv. That must be so hard on you." Nikki tries to step in to cover for her friend, but steps directly into my trap instead.

"Not really. The sex is even hotter now than it was before. We get along better than ever. In fact, he's grilling steaks for us tonight. I only ran out to grab a few things for dinner. That nudist colony we joined together has done wonders for our relationship. If either of you ever get married, I highly recommend you join too. It's only for married couples or I'd nominate you both right now."

"All right. Well. That sounds very... interesting. I'm glad to hear you and Ryder are doing so well. Nikki and I need to get going, but it was great seeing you." Cyndi and Nikki hurry off in the opposite direction as fast as their lying feet can move. Too bad it isn't as fast as their lying tongues can flap.

As I head back to Ryder's condo, I prepare to confess my subterfuge to him. Since the entire town will hear about our nudist colony membership by morning, with significant embellishments, I think I should at least give him a heads-up. When I finish recounting the entire story, Ryder stares at me with a completely blank expression for a moment. This is the only time I haven't been able to read his mind.

Then he bursts out laughing uncontrollably.

"Ry, did you dip into the chocolate edibles without me? Those were for the brownies, damn it." I put my hands on my hips, ready to fight. I've been looking forward to those chocolaty delights way too much.

"No. No, I haven't started without you. I just can't believe you felt threatened by Cyndi McNew. Maybe I should be offended because you think I'd be interested in having anything to do with her. Instead, I'm flattered you felt the need to stop her in her tracks."

"Threatened? Who said I was threatened by her?"

"You just did when you told me about making up a fake nudist colony you and I joined together. I couldn't care less what anyone says about me. But you just purposely started a new rumor about yourself, even though the gossip really bothers you. Liv, you threw yourself under the bus to keep her away from me."

The heat in his green eyes burns through my skin and touches my soul. They hold more than carnal desire though. He loves me with his entire being. Probably more than anyone will ever love me in my life. Not that there will be anyone after Ryder. Despite our differences, he's still my soul mate, and no one else can compete with him.

I'm playing with fire again, I know that. I'm not naïve or stupid. Extremely stubborn and thoroughly obstinate? Definitely. But I love the way Ryder burns me, and I can't seem to stay away from the flame.

"Can we eat soon? I'm famished." My words come out all breathy and sultry. He senses it too.

"I'm good to feast anytime you want, babe." He steps closer. "But the steaks will be ready in about eight minutes. Finish making our salads for us. I've got dessert covered."

"I'll be ready when you are. Don't worry about me."

"Oh, I'm counting on that promise. Don't let me down."

Captain Obvious in my mind points out we're not talking about the steaks anymore.

After dinner, we move to his back porch to relax and enjoy the crisp night air. The two-seat sofa is comfortable and inviting after a long, emotional day. Ryder sits beside me with a wide grin on his handsome face.

"Eat up while it's still warm." He passes the small plate over to me, and I eagerly take it.

One bite, and I'm in chocolate delight heaven. "You really know how to make me melt, Ry. Feed me a little chocolate and I become putty in your hands."

"Seems like I should've known that little secret about you a long time ago. If that's all it takes, I'll have you eating out of my hand in that nudist colony by the end of the night."

With an amused chuckle, I pop the last piece of

brownie in my mouth and settle against the back of the loveseat. Ryder points to a shooting star streaking across the dark sky, and I instinctively squeeze my eyes shut and make a wish. When I lean my head back again, it's against the crook of Ryder's shoulder.

This feels like home.

CHAPTER 10

Ryder

"How do you feel?" I ask with a smirk.

It's been about an hour since she ate two of my special brownies. I had to hide the rest of the pan before she devoured them all by herself. For the last few minutes, she's acted loopy and laughed at everything and nothing.

"So good. I feel more relaxed than I have in a long time. We should do this every week for the rest of our lives." She throws her arms out to the side in an exaggerated gesture, but she doesn't move from my arm otherwise.

"That may be a tad excessive for you, babe. You can barely hold your liquor." I chuckle good-naturedly, but I'm actually relieved to see her relaxing her tight grip on the control reins for once. "Just enjoy it for tonight."

"Thank you for taking care of me. You're still the best man I know."

I'd forgotten how marijuana loosened her tongue. Livvy has always been the type to keep her innermost thoughts and feelings to herself. That's how I know the therapy visits would be harder on her than she'd admit. My guess is she learned early to repress her feelings so she wouldn't be hurt by all the small-town gossip. By her admission earlier, she was only able to hide the pain, not avoid it.

"Can I ask you something, babe?"

"Of course. You can ask me anything. You know me better than anyone in the whole wide world." Her words suggest she's coherent, but she's feeling the full effects, judging by all the extra syllables and singsong voice she's using.

"How did we get so far off base with our life together? We always talked about traveling to different places and enjoying each other while we had time alone." Maybe it's unfair to ask her now, but I haven't been able to get a straight answer otherwise.

"Yes, we did plan that, but we were going to do it after we raised a family. You said you wanted a little girl like me and a little boy like you. We were going to have it all, you and me. But you changed our plans without talking to me first, Ry. If we leave here and travel around the world like your parents are doing, we won't have enough time left to have kids while we're young. We're already thirty years old. How much longer do you think we have to wait? I don't know of any way we can get what we want and still keep each other."

"Why is having children so important to you? We have each other, babe. We'll always have each other. Is it because all your friends have kids? Or because the people here expect it and look at you differently because we don't?"

"It has nothing to do with them, Ry. A baby would be a combination of you and me. A little piece of each of us that carries on long after we're gone. Something that ties us together for all eternity. Growing up as an only child was lonely most of the time. I want a house full of love, laughter, and happiness. But I only want that life with you, Ryder."

She leans over and lays her head on my lap. I push the hair out of her face, letting my fingers graze her skin. I'm too stunned and moved with emotion to speak at the moment, so I watch her in silence. She remembers exactly what I said about having kids while we were still in college. While part of me meant every word, another part spoke the words to be romantic. Fantasizing about our future was a fun pastime for two young adults who didn't have the extra money to do much more.

Her wealthy parents always tried to pay her way to make her life easier, but she rarely accepted their generosity. I thought her refusal of their help was strange at first. But then I got a closer look inside the Anderson household, and everything made so much more sense. As long as I've known them, her parents haven't been the affectionate type. They made appearances at special functions and supported Liv, but it always seemed to be from afar.

Too many people around here assumed she skated by on her family's wealth and connections, so she wanted to prove to herself and everyone else that she could be a success on her own accord.

"Your parents traveling all the time while you were growing up bothered you more than you ever showed me, didn't it?"

She turns on her side, giving me her back, and draws invisible circles on my leg. "Maybe."

"You never mentioned that to me, babe. Why'd you keep it from me?"

She lifts one shoulder, a vague response she gives when she doesn't want to talk about something. "Have you ever been afraid you'd fail at something you wanted more than anything?"

"Yes." I'm afraid I'll fail to stop this divorce. Terrified I'll lose you for good. Petrified of what I'll have to admit when the time comes.

"If I don't talk about how much something affects me, I don't have to deal with how disappointed I am when everything goes wrong."

I've gained more insight into her in one night than all our years together combined. Maybe we should do this once a week after all. Except, I may have cheated somewhat since I didn't eat any of the brownies and had no intention to partake from the start.

"Hey, I have another fun idea, if you're game." I rub the back of her neck, focusing on the knots in her muscles and the tight chords of ligaments and tendons.

"What's your idea?"

"Let's sneak out to old Mr. Davis's bridge and go skinny-dipping. It's late, so we should be the only ones out there. We'll start our own nudist colony in the woods here in Mason Creek."

"On one condition." I feel her cheek lift with her secret smile.

"Name it." Whatever her condition is, I'll meet it with bells on.

"Bring another brownie for us. I know you hid them. We need one for the road… or the trail. Whatever."

"You can have one more, but only after our swim. I don't want you passing out while we're in the water."

"Fine, but only because I'm not ready to go to sleep yet."

"Do you see anyone around?" She whisper-shouts at me, so if anyone is around, they absolutely know we're here too.

"I don't see anyone, babe. Do you really care if anyone else is here or not though?" I smile down at her, knowing she doesn't give a shit about anything tonight.

"Nope. Let's swim." She waggles her eyebrows at me, then lifts her shirt over her head. When she's stripped down to her birthday suit, she rushes to the water's edge and jumps in.

When she surfaces, she screams loudly.

"Did you forget how cold the water is?" I can't help but laugh as I shed my clothes and join her.

"I'm certain it's never been this cold before. We'll need a dip in a hot tub somewhere to thaw out after this." Her teeth chatter, but her happiness doesn't wane.

"If your lips turn blue, we're getting out."

"You'll have to drag me out of here." She jumps on me and pushes down on my shoulders until my head is underwater. She thinks she has the upper hand until I grab her around the ribs and start tickling her.

When I resurface, her squeals of laughter fill the air, echoing off the mountains and reverberating back to us. I wouldn't be surprised if the entire town heard her and came to investigate. Tonight, she wouldn't care if that happened, either.

Since we've caused enough ruckus for the night, I ease up on the torture and simply hold her in place instead. Then she wraps her legs around my waist and her arms around my neck. Water sloshes between us as she inches closer.

"This could be a very bad idea, Liv. You know what trouble this got us into last time." I'm trying to be a gentleman, but she's trying to have her way with me.

Only one of us can keep trying.

"You don't seem to have the problem of a cold-water willy tonight." She wiggles her hips against me. "Feels like Big Daddy Dong wants to play with me."

"There isn't a glacier in the world cold enough to quench my desire for you, babe. If we stay like this much longer, you'll have that hot tub you asked for earlier."

Her eyes drop to my mouth. Then her tongue darts out, wetting her lips.

There's no way we won't get busted for this. We'll be in the gossip column against first thing in the morning. By Monday morning, we'll have another conversation with Judge Nelson about why we're filing for a divorce when we keep getting caught having sex during our separation period. We'll wake tomorrow to another awkward encounter where we won't know how not to be with each other. This may even set us back further than we are now.

"I can read your mind, Ry. Stop overanalyzing everything. You're the one who encouraged me to relax and let go tonight. Now it's your turn. We'll deal with tomorrow when it gets here. Be here with me tonight though... wherever we are."

"That's the one thing you never quite got, babe."

"What's that?" Her lazy smile and bloodshot eyes are dead giveaways for how good she's feeling.

"You've never left my heart, so you're always with me... wherever I am."

"Why do you have to be so perfect for me?"

One side of my mouth lifts, and I shrug my shoulders. "Just comes naturally."

In slow motion, she tilts her head and covers my mouth with hers. I'm hers for the taking, and she eagerly takes me up on the offer. Despite the desperation building inside me, our movements are slow and purposeful. The longer I can keep her in my arms, the better. The more she turns to me, the closer we are to canceling our separation.

There's an answer to both our problems. We just haven't found it yet.

When she reaches her final release, she clutches me tightly and mutters in my ear, "Now, Ryder." Her sultry command is all the extra push I need to comply.

We swim, play, and laugh together for a while longer. Though it's summer, the nights still cool down significantly here, along with the water temperature. When her lips develop a blue tinge, I insist we dry off and head back to my place.

"Are you trying to trick me back into bed with you, Mr. King? I can see right through your games, you know."

"Bed? No, I wouldn't do that." I wink at her surprised expression. "But if I can entice you into a hot shower by plying you with liquor and brownies, I won't complain."

She slips her clothes on, wraps the towel around her shoulders, and steps under my arm. "A hot shower sounds perfect. You don't even have to drug me first."

"You partook more than willingly. You can't blame me for your food choices."

"I'm teasing, you know. I'd never do that. I'm right where I want to be, fully aware of what I'm doing.

You'd never take advantage of me like that and the whole town knows it."

We walk back to my condo with our arms wrapped around each other and our steps fall into perfect sync. Maybe our future is a little brighter after a skinny-dip under the starry sky. Maybe we can find a way through this mess together.

After a steaming hot shower for two, we fall into bed and fall asleep wrapped in each other's arms. Sheer exhaustion overtakes me almost as soon as my head hits the pillow. I think Liv was already half asleep before she even reached the bed. The last thing I hear before sleep pulls me into the darkness is the soft, rhythmic breathing of my wife in peaceful slumber.

The alarm goes off, and we groan in unison.

"I swear I just closed my eyes two seconds ago. How can it already be time to get up?" Liv grumbles into the pillow. Her voice is muffled, but my body echoes her sentiment.

"If we were independently wealthy, what would you do?"

She turns over to face me, laying her head on my chest. At least the awkwardness we felt last time is gone.

"I'd like to think I'd be this great humanitarian and philanthropist, but the truth is I'd probably do absolutely nothing." She chuckles at herself. "Sadly, we're not incredibly wealthy, so I have to get up and face the day. In our case, I'm afraid that also includes facing the music since everyone will know I'm here by now."

Annnd, the awkwardness is back.

"Are you working today?" I stroke her back with my fingertips, trying to keep the connection alive.

"No, I'm going to my parents' house today. They're on the way back from one of their whirlwind excursions. I'll get to spend time with Jeannine before they arrive. I've been extremely busy at the store lately, so I haven't seen her much at all."

"Can I ask you a question? You'd think I'd already know the answer, but I'm ashamed to admit I don't."

"Sure. Ask away." She acts like an open book, but I feel her protective walls rising into place.

"Last night you said you were lonely a lot while growing up. Was that because your parents left you behind while they went on their extended trips?"

She inhales deeply before answering. "Yes, that was a big part of it. They left me in Jeannine's care for weeks at a time. She did her best to entertain me and keep my mind off their absences, but I still felt it every time. I always thought it would be different if I had a bunch of siblings at home with me. But they never had other kids, so I always questioned if I was a mistake."

She's noticeably silent after blurting out her confession.

"I'm so sorry, babe. You never told me any of that before now. Sometimes I think I'm just now getting to know you, after all these years together. Why didn't you share any of this with me before now?"

She rests her chin on the back of her hand and looks up at me. "It wasn't that I was keeping anything from you, Ryder. Leaving the past behind me and focusing on our future was better for my own sanity. Besides, I never felt lonely or abandoned when we were together. You never made me think I was your biggest regret."

Her voice trails off, leaving the last words hanging in the air between us unspoken, but still as loud as thunder.

She never felt as if she was my biggest regret... until now.

CHAPTER 11

Olivia

"Jeannine, I'm home. Where are you? For crying out loud. Do I have to search every room? Where's the security around here? You just let anyone walk in off the street."

"No one would believe I taught you better than to scream throughout the house. They'll say I was a terrible nanny and shouldn't be allowed around children, all because of you." She steps out from the study into the large foyer with her arms folded across her chest.

"Don't give me that look, Neeny. It never worked on me as a child, so it definitely doesn't work on me now." I mimic her stance and initiate a staring contest.

She wins. I burst out laughing, as I always do. This

is a running gag between us. We've kept it going as far back as I can remember. She holds her arms open wide, and I rush into them without a second thought.

"Oh, my baby girl. I've missed you so much. You haven't come home in so long." She rocks from side to side, still holding me in her embrace as tightly as she can. "Why do I have to find out what's happening in your life through the gossip blogs instead of from you?"

"Ugh, that damn column. She means no harm, I know, but I hate being the flavor of the week." I rest my cheek on her shoulder and relish the affection from the only real mother I've had.

"Huh. Flavor of the week, nothing. You're the star of it again today." Her body shakes with laughter, and I bury my face. "Water was chilly, was it?"

"Not already. How could they possibly know? It was the freaking middle of the night—just a few hours ago."

She pushes me back to look at me. "Can't live with him but can't live without him, can you?"

"Something like that, I guess." I shrug and look down at the floor for a second, then meet her questioning gaze again. "That's not entirely true."

"Yeah, no shit, sweetheart. You two can't stay away from each other, and the whole town knows it. What else is going on in your glamours life that I don't know about?"

We walk into the kitchen and Jeannine makes us a cup of hot tea while I tell her all about my lingerie line and the magazine feature article coming out soon. She sits beside me, slides a cup in front of me, and grips my hand in hers.

"I had no idea those were all your designs, Liv. I'm so proud of you. Have you told Ryder the exciting news?"

"Um, no. I haven't told him any of it yet, Jeannine. What's wrong with me?" I blow on the tea and take a sip while she collects her thoughts.

"There's nothing wrong with you, sweetheart. You've always worked so hard to make everything you do absolutely perfect. I noticed it when you were a little child, always striving to impress your father with your drawings and anything else you made. It's not my place to say, but I always thought he was entirely too critical. Your mom and dad love and care about you, Liv. They just never learned how to show it the way they should." She slightly narrows her eyes, tilts her head to the side, and pats my hand.

Pity has always rubbed me the wrong way, but coming from Jeannine, it nearly tears my heart in two.

"I barely remember those times. Mostly, I just think about how often you were there for me."

"There's no doubt I always will be. Maybe you should allow your husband to do the same. He has supported you every step of the way so far. There's no reason to believe he'll stop."

"You mean other than that pesky divorce thing."

"Ah, yes, that. You're both clearly dead set on seeing that through. You barely speak. You can't even be in the same room as the other. Absolutely no love left between you two in the least." Her deadpan expression matches her monotone voice.

"You know, I can't quite put my finger on it, but it seems as if you're trying to tell me something. A secret, maybe? Feel free to be blunt and just put it out there."

"Olivia, you are making the biggest mistake of your life and only you can stop it." She leans in to hold my gaze with hers as she speaks.

"Gosh, it's just on the tip of your tongue, isn't it? Maybe you'll think of a way to phrase it soon." I rest my chin on my hand and give her my most innocent expression.

"Ryder King is a saint." She leans back, lowers her chin, and glares at me from under her furrowed brows. Then I slowly arch one eyebrow and smirk, waiting for her to read my mind. "Fine. Saint may be a little generous, considering the gossip I read this morning. But you still know what I meant."

"All right, I'm sensing a theme here. I had planned to avoid the gossip rag all together, but you're not going to let me. I suppose I should read it so I'll at least be prepared when I see the pointing fingers or hear the sniggers behind my back."

"And before your parents get home."

Begrudgingly, I pull up the *MC Scoop* on my phone. My initial reaction flies out of my mouth before I can stop it.

"Fucking hell!"

"I suggest a better explanation when your father questions you about it." Jeannine rinses out our cups and puts them in the dishwasher while I reread the article.

Rocky Mountain High

But we're not in Colorado, friends. This happened right here in Mason Creek.

Did anyone hear the shrieking mating call of the rare and elusive female kingfisher in the middle of the night?

We weren't magically transported to Africa by Puff the Magic Dragon. No, Scoopers, what you heard came from our very own naughty nightgown girl, Olivia King. She and her soon-to-be-ex-husband Ryder took to the river, high as a March kite, for a little late-night skinny-dipping.

From the sound of things, the water wasn't too cold for Mr. King, if you know what I mean. Does Mary Jane heighten the water experience? Nymph minds want to know.

For a couple going through a divorce, they definitely seem intent on keeping their relations open—way out in the open. With so many people trespassing on private land to reach the old bridge in the woods, the owners installed a few security cameras for their own protection.

No word yet on if Mrs. King's fishing expedition landed her a whopper, but it does appear Mr. King can't resist the bait she dangles in front of him. He's caught in her trap —hook, line, and, per the Mrs. herself—a nudist colony membership. Although, for those of you who frequent her shop, you're already mostly nude, anyway!

Stay tuned for more as the latest on the Ex Marks the Spot segment unfolds.

"Jeannine, the only merciful action to take now is to kill me. Put me out of my misery and help me avoid the repercussions yet to come." I stare at my phone, still in disbelief, as she sits next to me again.

"Look at me, Olivia." She waits for my full attention. "No."

"No, what?"

"No, I won't save you from yourself this time. You're a grown woman. You only answer to those whom you choose."

"You're right. Yeah. Yeah. You're exactly right. I'm going to use this free publicity to my advantage. My 'Draw the Shades' premier night will be the talk of the town for so many reasons. In fact, I'm even more excited about it now than ever before." I jump up from my seat, throw my arms around her neck, and place a long, hard kiss on her cheek. "Thank you, Momma Neeny. I love you."

"I love you too, baby girl. Go show everyone how a real woman roars. Or squeals, in your case."

Our shared laughter quickly dies with the sound of the door from the garage slamming shut.

"I'm glad you're here." Dad sounds anything but glad. His loud, gruff voice holds more irritation than usual. His eyes burn with anger, all directed at me. His lips form a thin line as he paces back and forth, all while staring holes through me.

This stance used to intimidate me. But not today. My epiphany only a moment ago revealed more to me than a robust marketing plan ever could. My life is mine to live. My choices are mine to make. My accomplishments are mine to be proud of and celebrate. My worth is mine to decide.

"Really? Because you don't sound glad. That's unfortunate, since I bet you couldn't tell me when the last time you saw me was. Let's double down on that bet while we're at it. When was the last time you were glad to see me?"

My outburst surprises him. He stops pacing in mid-stride and jerks backward, as if I physically slapped him. His bottom jaw drops open, and for a few seconds, he reminds me of a fish. His mouth opens as if he'll say something, then closes again without making a sound. His stiff arms drop to his sides, hanging loose in an uncharacteristic display of sloppy demeanor.

"Your mother and I were... shocked to read about you in the local gossip column. Not once, but twice. Care to explain yourself?" He raises his eyebrows and purses his lips.

"Nope."

"Beg your pardon?"

"No, I do not care to explain myself, my actions, my marriage, or my business to anyone. If this is the first time you've heard rumors about me, you obviously haven't paid attention over my entire life. This article is one of a thousand rumors spread all over town about me. I don't owe you an explanation for this one any more than I owe you one for any other tale about me."

"Then why are you here?" Mom looks genuinely confused. I could almost get past her question easier if it was asked out of anger or frustration, but not this.

"That's a great question, Mom. Why am I here? Am I the mistake you couldn't make right? Was I an accident you never intended to take responsibility for? Only you can answer the question about why I'm here."

"We did not raise you to speak to us this way." She puts her fists on her hips and glares in my direction, but she can't quite make eye contact with me.

"You're right, you didn't. Because you didn't raise me at all. Jeannine did. And when she was off work, the other members of the house staff stepped in. But you? No, you didn't raise me to speak to anyone like this. But since I'm grown and have made my own way without your help, I'm free to tell the harsh truth."

"Well, if that's how you feel about us..."

"Well, if that's all you have to say about my existence in your lives and about being my parents..."

The heavy pause in the conversation reveals as much as their words did.

"Since my presence in my parents' home is such a

mind-boggling mystery, I won't be back until the reasons become clear. Or, I should say, *if* the reasons ever become clear."

Jeannine had left the room during our confrontation, but now she waits by the front door, her face beaming with pride. "I know that was hard for you, sweetheart, but you did the right thing. Confront your fears and demons head-on. Stop letting them bully you."

"Did you just call my parents demons?"

"Yes, I sure did."

We muffle our laughter as we say goodbye, then I head back to my house. I have a lot of work to do if I'm going to pull off this fashion show anytime soon. And since the big day will be here in only six weeks, I have to get my idle ass in gear. No more lazing about with happy brownies and tequila shots.

After several hours of developing a solid fashion show outline, identifying the perfect models, and finding all the supplies I'll need to succeed in this enormous undertaking, I'm finally ready to begin making outreach calls. Except now it's almost eleven o'clock at night, and none of the local stores are open. When I stand from my drawing board, I feel every one of my thirty years in my aching muscles and frozen joints.

That soak in a hot tub would be perfect right about now.

Since I can't start at the top of my to-do list, I grab the large box of men's underwear samples from the manufacturer. I'm always so excited to see my new creations come to life every time a new shipment arrives. This one is especially exciting because it makes a distinct new line and new direction for my little company.

One by one, I hold up the new garments, inspecting every seam and how the fabric of choice hangs. Visual presentation is paramount to selling the inventory, especially around here where all the men are more rough-and-rowdy than *GQ*-and-cultured. They need more than a nudge in the right direction. They have to be pushed off the cliff with their four-wheel-drive truck, holding a beer and scratching their ass on the way down.

On that note, another idea strikes me like lightning out of nowhere. My fashion show is incomplete, and there's only one way to remedy it. Lucky for me, this will have everyone's tongues wagging about my shop, my show, and my talent. For once, I may just have the perfect excuse to make them talk about me.

But this reason will remain my secret—and mine alone—until party night. Then it's go time.

CHAPTER 12

Ryder

Therapy session number two is today, and I feel like I need it more than ever. It's been a week since our last session—and our last night together—but I haven't heard from Liv since then. Here I thought we'd turned a new corner and could put all this unpleasantness behind us. Instead, she disappeared for an entire week without so much as a kiss my ass on her way out of my life once more.

Kiwi and I arrive for our appointment a few minutes early. Allie greets us and ushers us into her office. Again, Liv isn't here yet, opting for a fashionably late entrance instead. Maybe she's not taking this part of the process as seriously as I am. Allie could help us work through the invisible baggage cluttering our relationship if we'd both just lay all our issues on the line.

With two minutes to spare, Liv rushes into the room and sits beside me as she did last time. She's barely seated, but she's bouncing up and down, unable to sit still. Her face beams with happiness, and her smile splits her face in two. She hasn't spoken a word yet, but her obvious excitement is contagious, nonetheless.

"What has gotten into you?" I'm trying to play it cool, but I'm dying to know what's going on.

"You!" She releases a little squeal before grabbing my hand. "You had the best idea ever. I've spent the last seven days and nights planning every single detail of my upcoming fashion show. I'm so excited. I can hardly wait."

"That's great news, Olivia." Allie claps enthusiastically. "You said Ryder gave you the idea?"

"Yes, he did. I'm very impressed with his suggestion too since he never really took any interest in growing my business before. But this was pure genius. So, I've been working night and day to plan, prepare, and order everything I'll need so it arrives before the big event. I'm calling it the 'Draw the Shades' night. The theme will be living the high life. I've never been so tired and so energized at the same time." She turns to me again and squeezes my hand.

"Why do you think Ryder wasn't interested in your business? Did he say or do something to give you that impression?" Allie's listening and using the pieces of the story to bring us back to the point of the session. I get that. But she's being a total buzzkill right now.

"Well, he never really talked about it or asked me how it was doing past the usual 'how was your day' conversations. When I first opened the store, I'd try to give him all the details, but I learned quickly not to bother. He only half-listened or changed the subject entirely. So, it became my business instead of ours." She moves her hand back to her lap.

"Did you ever ask him why he wasn't engaged in it?"

"Yes. Maybe not in those words, but the sentiment was the same. I don't remember what he said exactly, but my gut reaction was he was embarrassed by my choice of livelihood as much as my parents were."

My head jerks in her direction without conscious thought of it. I never knew her parents were embarrassed by her business.

"That must've been hard for you, living with that constant scrutiny in the back of your mind." Allie's empathy is genuine, as is my utter shock. "Ryder, do you want to address her feelings?"

"Babe, I never knew that. You never told me." I'm still floored and not sure how to respond.

"Why would I, Ryder? You didn't care. If you'd paid attention, you would've noticed. But you felt the same as they did, so you looked the other way. My store may be unconventional as far as small towns go, but my merchandise has saved or breathed new life into countless relationships around here. I have nothing to be sorry about. I bet you can't say the same though."

"You're right. I should've been more supportive. In fact, I realized that the other night after our talk. There are a lot of things I should've done differently. Had I known how much the gossip affected you, I would've demanded they stop. "

"Oh, please. They won't stop just because Ryder King demands it. But you could've supported me through it much better than you did." She fires her words back at me, aiming for my heart.

"You're absolutely right, and I'll own that. If I'd looked in the mirror and realized how much of an ass I was, I could've done a lot of things differently. But you weren't the easiest person to be married to either, you know. All our problems weren't because of me." I lean forward in my seat, preparing for battle.

"Can you elaborate on that statement, Ryder?" Allie probes harder.

"Oh yeah, I can elaborate all right. With pleasure. Liv is a *TV show cheater* who has no regard for anyone else."

"I'm sorry. She's a what?"

"She's a TV show cheater. We agreed to watch the *Game of Thrones* series together. No watching ahead when the other wasn't around. No bingeing in secret. But she'd watch entire seasons while I was away,"

"You went hunting every weekend and for a solid week in the fall with the guys. It was cold and snowing, and I was home alone. You were off having fun without me, so I watched our show. I still watched it again with you."

"And told me all the plot points before I saw them for myself. You're a walking TV show spoiler alert." I point at her to emphasize my point.

"At least I'm not embarrassed of you, even though you still can't put the dishes in the right spot when you empty the dishwasher. It's not like they haven't been in the same damn spot for seven fucking years."

"All right, guys, let's get back to the feelings behind those aggravations rather than the acts themselves. Ryder, why does it bother you when Liv watches the show without you?" Allie tries to get us back on track again, but my feathers are still ruffled.

"It makes me feel angry."

"I got that, but why? Dig deeper."

With an exaggerated sigh, I let go of some of my irritation. "Because that was supposed to be our time together. We could experience the shocking revelations at the same time and talk about them afterward. That was our special time, and we didn't have enough of that."

Allie nods, both in understanding and in appreciation for my honesty.

"Olivia, you mentioned the embarrassment issue again after Ryder said he'd own it, so I think we need to explore that a little more. It obviously still bothers you."

"Of course it still bothers me. How would you feel if the love of your life, your husband until death parts you, can't even introduce you to new people out of fear they'll ask what you do for a living? It's bullshit."

"Why did you stay with him, knowing that?"

"Because I love him, and my store isn't as important as he is. Marriage requires a lot of forgiveness, every day."

"Then what pushed you to the point of filing for a divorce?"

Here we go.

"We were arguing over what color to paint the spare bedrooms one day. He always starts a fight then blames me for it. Anyway—"

"I do not start fights. You start them then tell everyone I did."

"Anyway, as I was saying before I was so rudely interrupted, we were redecorating the spare bedrooms, and I mentioned it was time to make one of them into a nursery. You would've thought I'd asked him to donate a spare testicle to my gender reassignment operation. He lost all composure and eventually confessed he doesn't want children. He wants to sell everything we own and travel the world instead. As if everything we own would finance that trip for more than a few months. Then we'd come back to—what? Absolutely nothing.

"A stable, mentally healthy grown man doesn't think in those absurd terms. He's having a midlife crisis or something along those lines at thirty years old. But he doesn't want to stay here. He doesn't want a family. And he doesn't want to make a life with me. We've hit a brick wall and there's no other way around this than to go our separate ways."

"Is that how you feel, Ryder? That divorce is the only answer?" Allie rounds her desk and sits on the front of it, between Liv and me.

"No, I've never believed that. Despite the six million things about Liv that drive me absolutely insane, I think our love can overcome anything. She's the one who decided what I want is absurd and what she wants is all that matters. She's the one who dumped me like yesterday's garbage when she didn't get what she wanted. But then, our whole relationship has been about what she wants. Where we went to college, where we lived, and now, the fate of the rest of our lives." I cut my eyes over to Liv and my heart skips a beat.

"That's not fair, Ryder. We chose the college we *both* got into. If you wanted to go somewhere else, you should've spoken up. We moved back here because this is our home. Where else did you want to go? If you insisted that we move anywhere else, I must've been asleep. And as far as where you work, that arrangement was made with your parents, not me. How can you blame me for all your choices?"

"Because you wouldn't have gone along with my choices, Liv. You would've told me to go live my best life without you." I don't know when I stood up, but now I'm pacing the length of the room, wondering how we're at the boiling point of tempers when she was so happy and grateful just a few minutes ago.

"You never gave me an opportunity, though, did you? Instead, you made that decision for me, then blamed me for it every day since." She's quiet for a minute while I stare at the ceiling. "Allie, tell me something. How can any couple stay together when one of them has so much hidden resentment and embarrassment toward the other? What hope could they possibly have?"

"Oh, you'd be surprised, Olivia. Sometimes this process feels like we're reopening old wounds and pouring salt directly into them. But we have to dig into what caused those wounds before we can heal them. If you commit to doing just that, you can come out stronger and better healed on the other side. We're not as concerned with who's at fault as we are with how we can get closure for those wounds."

Allie moves back to her seat behind the desk and retrieves her calendar. Our time today is almost up, and I feel further away from Liv than ever. Yeah, I heard her explanation and I understand we have to deal with our problems to get past them. This feels more like we're getting ready to say goodbye and preparing our hearts for the final fracture.

"I have the same day and time open next week. Will that still work for you both?" She looks between us, waiting for an answer like she didn't just start World War III.

"Fine," we reply at the same time, making us finally meet each other's gaze.

"I'm sorry I made you feel like I was ashamed of you. If I could go back and change every time that you felt that way because of me, I'd do it in a heartbeat. But all I can do is swear I'll never make you feel that way again."

Tears well in her eyes, but she quickly swallows her emotions, pushing them back down past the lump in her throat. "Thank you for saying that, Ry. This has been an especially emotional week, after a confrontation with my parents, another article about me, and a new step in my business. Then today."

"What happened when you saw your parents?" This can't be good.

She glances at Allie, who's fully invested in our conversation now, then turns her attention back to me. "Maybe we should walk and talk. We've taken up enough of Allie's time for today."

"Good idea. I know just the place where we won't be interrupted. We probably won't even see another person."

"That sounds exactly like what I need right now. Let's go."

As we say goodbye to Allie, I catch of glimpse of her in therapist mode, observing and studying how we interact. When she realizes I've caught her, she quickly schools her features and straightens her already crisp clothes. Now I wonder if we're being observed when we don't realize it. Is she reading the local tabloids too?

Liv and I walk together on the sidewalk outside the doctor's office and Kiwi hops over to Liv's shoulder. When we reach my truck, I open her door and help her in. On the way to the mountains, we keep the conversation light and easy, mostly talking about Kiwi and how busy Liv's been the past week. Focusing on the topics that bring her peace will hopefully make the rest of our evening easier on her.

When I park at the trailhead, she looks over her shoulder at me with a smile. "You hate hiking this trail."

"But you love it."

With Liv on my arm and Kiwi on hers, we set off into the woods together. She begins telling me about her visit with her parents and how hurtful and disappointing it turned out for her. But for me, I'm completely livid. The only reason I'm not beating down their door to throttle them right now is because of the beautiful lady at my side. She deserves all my attention and support.

A single tear falls from her eye as she finishes the story about their encounter. She quickly wipes it away. Then she slides her arm around my waist and steps closer to me. Our feet fall in step as we stroll along the empty trail, taking our time and enjoying the company in silence. My arm encircles her shoulders.

"What can I do to make it better?" I lean over and kiss the top of her head, leaving my lips there for the connection.

"You're already doing it. Just being here for me is enough." She squeezes me in her way of saying thank you without saying a word.

"Give me a kiss, baby." Kiwi bends her head to the side when she looks at me. "Big kiss."

"Where is she learning these crazy phrases? She's

been saying all kinds of things to me lately." I lean down and give Kiwi a kiss on her beak as she demanded.

"I have no idea, but she's been saying unusual phrases to me too. One time she asked, 'is she gone yet?' She has even tried to whisper. Made me wonder if your girlfriend had been teaching my bird naughty words."

"My girlfriend?" I laugh out loud at that notion. "You're the only one for me, babe. Always have been. Always will be."

She halts our steps and looks up at me. Her deep blue eyes burn into my soul. There's a definite longing in there, but it's deeper than physical intimacy. She's craving the emotional intimacy only our love provides. She wants to say something, but she's holding herself back. Her lips part and close. The anticipation is quickly replaced with hesitancy. But I can wait. It's on the tip of her tongue.

"Momma, kiss Daddy." Kiwi deserves another treat.

"Yeah, Momma. Kiss Daddy." My invitation is wide open.

CHAPTER 13

Olivia

"No. No. No. Not again. This can't be happening." Three text message alerts set the tone for my day. They came in one after the other, all from different people, asking if the newest article posted on the *MC Scoop* blog is true.

"What's wrong, babe?" Ryder raises his head from under his pillow to see what I'm freaking out about now.

"Apparently, I'm the hot topic of the *MC Scoop* again today. At this point, I'm almost afraid to read it. The last two articles were so flattering, after all." I roll my eyes. "Tate must like you. She always makes you sound like a sex god while I'm the queen of the Jezebels."

"A sex god, huh? I like the sound of that. Maybe you can scream it for me later." He wraps his arm around my waist and pulls me back down on the bed with him. "Or right now. Or now and later."

"What do you think she's saying about me this time? Everyone in a twenty-mile radius knows your truck has been in my driveway since our last therapy appointment seven days ago. What could possibly be news today? We haven't bothered anyone."

"Who cares what she writes, Liv? I sure as hell don't. It's almost as bad as being back in high school. We left all that stupid bullshit behind a long time ago. Even if I closed my store and spent every second of every day with my wife in her lingerie store, it's no one else's business. We can live our life however we want."

"You're right. It just seems like they'd get tired of talking about us and move on to something that matters. Why so many people are invested in our marriage is beyond me."

"I'm just glad you're still invested in it. I don't give a shit if anyone else is."

"I'm not even going to read it. Whatever it says isn't worth my energy or the frustration it'll cause. We deserved this time off together after everything we've been through."

Our impromptu vacation was exactly what we needed. Our employees are more than capable of running the stores while we're away. They also know all they have to do is call if an emergency arises. We've allowed everyone and everything else to run our lives, except ourselves.

After the last visit with my parents, I realized something important about myself and about Ryder. Throughout all the years since my parents moved us here to give me a small-town childhood, everyone thought my life was so easy and glamourous. My wealthy parents were always on one extravagant trip or another. The times they took me with them was to keep up the appearance of a happy family.

But they never truly wanted me. All I wanted was their love, but they can't give what they don't possess. Even as a kid, I knew I was a burden to them. A small-town childhood simply meant their jet-setter friends didn't see their apathy toward me. No brothers or sisters confirmed I was their biggest mistake. I've always known, but I never had the courage to confront the truth until now.

Ryder, on the other hand, has been by my side since we were kids in elementary school. We've been friends, lovers, and soul mates, even amid all the pain and turmoil. We've aggravated each other to no end, but we always end up back in each other's arms. The love and belonging I tried to find in my family was never lacking in my relationship with Ryder.

My epiphany was simultaneously simple and profound. Everything I learned about love, I learned from Ryder. From the way he loves me to the things he does for me without my asking. By the way he takes care of me when I'm sick, starts my car when it's cold, and brings me lunch when I'm busy at the store. I learned how to love and be loved in every little and grand gesture my husband has ever done for me and for us.

During our walk in the woods, he apologized profusely for making me feel as if he was anything remotely like my parents. He assured me he wasn't ashamed or embarrassed by me or my work in the least. Owning two businesses trapped us here, and he feared we'd never get out of the rut.

I tried to tell him about my big news and how it may change our lives, but he wouldn't let me finish. "No more talking about work or anything else outside this forest," he said. Shielding us from the stressors in the world seemed important to him, so I dropped the subject for the time being. We've barely left the house over the last week while we continued to avoid any real-life problems.

"Now that we're wide awake, I should get up and make you some breakfast. We have another thrilling therapy session today." Ryder rolls out of bed and strolls through the bedroom, completely naked.

"We don't have to talk to her if we tell her we decided to stop the divorce."

He stops in his tracks and stares at me with a mixture of hope and fear in his eyes. "Are you serious, babe? Don't fuck with me about this."

"I wouldn't do that to you. Not about something as important as this. You know I love you more than life itself. How am I supposed to live without you?"

"What about our irreconcilable differences?" He steps toward me, tentatively but also hopeful.

"Help me understand why you're so opposed to having a family. Don't give me some unattainable dream of traveling the world with no money in our pocket. But I do want to hear the truth of what's in your mind and your heart." I pat the empty space beside me.

He sits and turns toward me, taking my hand in his. "It's not that I don't want a family, exactly. My parents ran the jewelry store their entire lives. They barely scraped by when they first started it. We had no family vacations, other than camping in our backyard for a weekend. There was no room for any luxury items—only the bare necessities. When it finally started to turn a profit, they were ecstatic.

"Still, scholarships paid for my education. My parents were able to make small investments over the years that paid off. Plus, they sold the business to me before they moved away, so now they're free. No kids at home. No business to stress over. They travel from place to place, working seasonal jobs when they need extra money. But other than that, they're not tied down by anything."

"You think a family would tie us down? You don't see any benefits to having children?" I'm struggling to understand his hesitation, but I'm still trying.

He shrugs nonchalantly, but a grimace covers his face. He runs his hand through his hair and doesn't meet my eyes. "Maybe."

That's a definite no to having a family.

"Okay, I suggest we talk to Allie today about helping us work through this as a team. If we continue on this path, one of us will be disappointed, maybe even resentful. We'll have to find a way to deal with it, one we can both live with and not let it cause more problems."

Most of the dealing, disappointment, and resentment will be on my part. I realize that, since I'll be the one forced to relinquish my needs so we can stay together. The combined visit will allow Ryder and me to address issues together and keep us on the same page.

His face falls as realization sets in. "How can I be happy when I'm asking you to give up everything you want so I can have what I want?"

"I don't have any answers, Ry. What's your plan? Sell both our businesses, the house, the condo, everything, to travel the world? What about Kiwi?"

"We don't have to sell our businesses. We'll turn the day-to-day operations over to a full-time store manager and keep paying ourselves a salary. Kiwi can travel with us. We've always moved her around. I think she'll be fine as long as she's with us. Maybe we start by touring places we want to see in the US before we take her on any international trips. Get her used to being in new places every week."

"What if it stresses her out, and she starts pulling out her feathers? What then?"

His eyes drift to the spot above my head where Kiwi sits on the headboard. Concern fills his eyes as he reaches up to scratch her. "Then we'll come home and take care of her. I don't want to hurt her."

"I know you don't. You mentioned making breakfast, right? I'll get dressed, then make her meals and treats for the day. We can go for another long walk if you want. It's nice to get away from everyone for a while. At least until our appointment time, anyway."

"Sounds like a plan to me. The food will be ready by the time you get out of the shower." His voice and his eyes seem detached, despite his attempt to appear otherwise.

We're still skating on thin ice, though we're treading carefully.

We walk into Allie's office together, without Kiwi this time, and she immediately raises her eyebrows. "What's going on here?"

"After our last session, Ryder and I spent a lot of time talking about the issues that were discussed. We went for a hike on my favorite trail and enjoyed spending time together, removed from the rest of the world. Then we spent the last week in a continued therapy session of our own making. We've been able to reconnect in a way we'd forgotten about for so long—just the two of us."

"I feel a 'but' coming on. Is this a good place for it?" Allie's eyes dart between us, waiting for the other shoe to drop.

"Yeah, about that..." Ryder starts to speak, then hesitates. "But... we still want different things out of life. So one of us has to give up our dreams to make the other happy. Except neither of us can be happy in that case. How can I live with myself knowing I took Liv's dreams of being a mother away from her?"

"Because we both feel the same about that, we thought it would be a good idea to continue our therapy sessions to help us navigate through these obstacles in our marriage. We both need to find ways to accept the sacrifices staying together will take." When I reach to hold Ryder's hand, the expression on his face startles me.

His brows are furrowed, his eyes are narrowed, and his mouth gapes open. I honestly have no idea what he's suddenly so pissed about, but I haven't seen him this mad in years.

"Sacrifices? Did you just saying keeping our marriage alive requires sacrifices on your part?"

"I didn't mean just me. But yes, I will have to sacrifice my needs and my desires and my dreams so you can have yours. I don't understand why that makes you mad. It's simply the truth, and deep down, you know it."

"When we got married, I don't remember our vows including promising to keep you barefoot, pregnant, and pampered. I remember for better or worse. I remember promising to love each other, come what may. There was no one else in that equation, not even kids. But now you have to *sacrifice* everything to be with me, as if I'm the bad guy here and you're the saint. As if I went back on my word and abandoned you."

"What word would you use instead of sacrifice, Ryder?" Allie interjects, and I'm thankful because I'm stunned speechless.

"I don't know. Adjustments, maybe. A change of expectations, even if they were her own and nothing we agreed to do together. But now I think it's pretty clear how she views our marriage. She doesn't have to make any sacrifices at the great altar of Ryder King. I'll be just fine without her burnt offerings." He spits out the last few words with such venom, it makes me recoil in my chair. He flies out of his seat and paces the room.

"Ryder, I think you may be overacting slightly. You just told me Liv would have to give up what she wants to be with you. That's the same thing as sacrificing her needs. You're getting hung up on semantics. She's here, isn't she?" Allie stands and moves to block Ryder's path. "I think there's something else bothering you, but you've latched on to this morsel to avoid the rest of the truth. Are you threatened by the news in the *MC Scoop* more than you want to admit, or have you withheld something more substantial from Liv?"

"What news?" Ryder and I ask at the same time.

Allie's head quickly jerks between the two of us. Her bottom jaw hangs open, and her eyes are as big as saucers. "Have you really not read it? Everyone in town has been talking about it all day. I'm sorry. I thought you both knew."

"I knew there was another article about me because three of my friends sent me texts first thing this morning. All they asked was if it was true. I assumed it was another update about Ryder and me."

Allie slowly shakes her head. "No, Olivia. That's not what this one is about. I'm truly sorry. It was inappropriate of me to assume, and you both have my sincere apologies."

Ryder and I fish our phones out of our pockets at the same time and pull up Tate's blog. If it's not about Ryder's truck being in my driveway over the last week, day and night, I'm afraid of what else she could've written about. The headline doesn't bode well for us.

CHECKMATE.
QUEEN TAKES KING.
GAME OVER.

Isn't a king supposed to protect his queen? It seems the King of Mason Creek has left his queen on her own too long. She found a new pastime to keep her busy day and night, and the outside world is taking notice.

Yes, Scoopers, this article is about our very own Olivia King again, but we've moved past her pending divorce misadventures. She's stepping up and stepping out—in her unmentionables!

The world-renown high fashion magazine Entranced recently discovered the Roots & Wings lingerie brand we MCers have loved for years. But it seems our queen has been keeping a rather large secret from all of us. Not only is Queen's Unmentionables the sole store that carries the Roots & Wings brand, but our very own Liv King designed every piece herself— from sketch to production.

Now that Entranced magazine editors have fallen head over heels in love with the designs and the designer, they've announced an enormous world-wide giveaway to promote Liv's small business and make her a household name.

Since this has to be the best-kept secret in Mason Creek, we have to ask the obvious question first.

Did Mr. King know Mrs. Queen was the brains and the talent?

With such obvious ability and considerable backing for her secret endeavor, how much longer do we expect her to stick around this sleepy little town? The bright lights of the world's most famous fashion shows will be clamoring to work with our girl before long.

The Queen is going places.

Will our King be Queen-less? Where does that leave him? Manning the panty store while the missus makes the big bucks and the executive decisions?

This Queen has proven she's the most valuable piece on the board, and she's playing to win.

Checkmate, indeed.

Check your mate, friends. Check your mate.

You never know what they may be hiding under their clothes.

Maybe they have Roots & Wings.

My hands shake, my heart pounds, and the blood rushes through my ears so loudly I can barely hear much else. No one from the magazine gave me advance notice about this giveaway and the resulting media buzz it has caused. Not that I know of, anyway, since I've been off the grid with Ryder long enough to have missed too much.

"Is this true, Olivia?" Ryder rarely uses my full name. He uses Liv or Livvy interchangeably, though it's Livvy when he's being especially affectionate. He almost never says Olivia though. "Have you been hiding this from me the entire time you've had your store?"

"Yes, it's true. I actually started in college with my sorority sisters and their friends. The lingerie in my store is mine and always has been. It's one of the reasons why I'm so proud of it, and why I'm so offended when my family acts embarrassed by it."

Before I finish speaking, he slams the door on his way out.

CHAPTER 14

Ryder

The door slams hard on my exit, shaking the wall and startling the others in the doctor's office. But I don't give a shit about any of them. I've been the loving and supportive partner for years. After college graduation, I moved back here despite my strong personal objections and best intentions to make a new life for us somewhere else.

Every day, I've gone to work in the jewelry store and went home to my wife every night. The same grind, day in and day out. Keeping both our businesses going has been the focal point of our existence. And the only piece of repetitiveness keeping me afloat was knowing one day all our hard work would pay off and we could implement my plan to get out.

Now to find out Liv has been building a secret business—one that could be done from anywhere in the world—feels like the final nail in our relationship's coffin. She hid this part of herself from me since before we were even married. She said this started in college and just grew from there.

Do I even know her anymore?

Did I ever?

Why would she hide something so important from me, of all people?

Without conscious thought of where I should go, my feet carry me to Pony Up. Perfect. I could use a beer or twelve to numb this giant crack in my heart. Liv was supposed to be my soul mate. My forever and ever.

I sidle up to the bar and take the first stool I come to. The bartender raises his brows and jerks his chin up.

"Beer with a shot of whiskey, and don't let either glass go dry."

He nods, understanding etched in his features, as he pours the first round. "Your day's been that good, huh?"

"Better, actually." I throw back the shot and drain the beer mug in a fast chug. "Hit me again."

He looks unsure, but does as I ask anyway, albeit slower this time. His tactics don't slow me down though. Once again, I finish off both drinks in record time and order a third.

"You need to slow down, Ryder. You're drinking a lot of alcohol in a short time. That's exactly how you get alcohol poisoning. Especially since you aren't in here all the time. You have no tolerance built up to it. I can't serve you another one yet, man. Not in good conscience." He steps back from the bar and crosses his arms.

I may be a little buzzed from guzzling, but I'm not inebriated. As of now, my anger is keeping me sober.

"Joe. Dude. I'm fine. I'm an adult. A grown man. I can make my own decisions. Give me another beer and another shot. Right now." I pound the bar with my fist.

He stares at me with his brows furrowed and a serious expression on his normally friendly face. When I don't back down, he relents. "Fine. One more. That's it for a while." He places them in front of me and walks off.

I shoot the whiskey but drink the beer a little slower this time. All I want is to numb the pain and stop the thoughts that are running rampant through my mind. Then I feel a hand grip my shoulder before Grayson slides onto the stool beside me.

"What's going on, Ryder?" Grayson has been my best friend for too long to let me get away with shit.

"You read Tate's article?" I lift the mug to my mouth and drain it.

"Yeah, I read it."

"That's how I found out my wife has a secret clothing line business and has been recognized by *Entranced* magazine. Not because she trusted me enough to be her partner in everything that affects our lives. Not because she loves me enough not to keep life-changing secrets from me. But because our local gossip queen revealed my wife's secret life to the whole town —including me." I hold up my empty mug and point to it with my other hand. Our friendly neighborhood bartender doesn't look pleased.

"Have you asked Liv why she didn't confide in you when this first started?" Grayson's even-keel tone usually calms me and helps me look at the problem from a different angle. It's the dad in him, remaining calm until he has all the facts. But tonight, I need to let my anger out or I'll explode like a keg of dynamite.

"No, I didn't ask because nothing she says will make it okay. This little revelation has made me question our entire relationship, and just when we were well on our way to reconciling for good. She should've told me." My glass is still empty. "Joe, I will climb over this bar and refill this mug myself if you don't get your ass over here."

"It's okay, Joe. I'll babysit him." Grayson only

laughs harder when I flip him off. "Ryder, what did Liv say about it?"

I repeat her confession word for word to Grayson, adding that's when I walked out. "I'm not going back, either. Fuck therapy. Fuck marriage. Fuck the lies."

"Yeah, that's the alcohol talking, all right. The Ryder King I know would stop to consider both what his wife said and what she didn't say before making that kind of declaration." Grayson arches one brow at me.

"What do you mean?" The full effects of the copious amount of liquor and beer are hitting me now.

"Look, you don't want to admit the truth because you feel bad about it. But we both know you were embarrassed when she announced her business. You wanted to hide in a hole. I was with you, if you remember. Don't you think she sensed that in you, even if you didn't come right out and say it? She knows you inside and out."

"I thought I knew her inside and out too."

"Ryder, she told you why she's so sensitive about her business. You told me all about that conversation she had with you. Everyone wants their business to succeed—even you. But you don't design every piece of jewelry in your store. You didn't put your heart and soul into creating something you hope others love. Until you put your heart out there for the entire town to trample on, you can't judge her." Grayson sits back and folds his arms across his chest.

"You're taking her side? She intentionally left me out of a huge part of her life." My argument makes sense to me.

"And you took away something important to her, but she was willing to let it go so you two can stay together. There's more to that part of the story, but you're not telling anyone. Most men don't just up and decide not to have a family with the woman they love. Not without an in-depth conversation about it, anyway. But you just unilaterally snatched it out from under her after seven years of marriage. What kind of partner does that make you?" His comments hit the mark a little too close to the truth for my comfort.

He's learned the art of patience with his twin four-year-old girls. He remains silently staring at me until I relent.

"All right, fine. You want the ugly truth of the matter? Here it is. I'm not even sure I can have kids. I've been to the doctor and had some tests done. He said it's not impossible, but not likely. You don't think it kills me not to be able to give my wife what she wants more than anything?"

"Shit, man, I'm sorry. What made you even question it?"

"Liv and I weren't careful about not getting pregnant for a long time. At first, I thought it was just pure dumb luck. But the longer we went, the more suspicious I became something was wrong. Turns out, I was right."

"Let me guess. You never told Liv about this little problem. Did you?"

"No, I couldn't bring myself to break it to her. It's bad enough being disappointed every time I look in the mirror. I don't think I could take the same expression in her eyes when she looks at me." Just thinking about it makes me cringe.

"She loves you, Ryder. You're being way harder on yourself than she ever would be. She'd support you without a second thought. Besides, there are other ways to put a baby in her belly. You still get to have all the fun and all the benefits of it too. Don't count yourself out so easily."

I hate when he's right.

Joe returns to our end of the bar with two fresh beers. He sets them in front of us and walks away without a word. I turn my attention back to Grayson. "What are you doing here, anyway? Where are my girls?"

"I heard you were here, drowning your sorrows a little too enthusiastically, and knew I'd better get over here to check on you myself. Your girls are spending a little quality time with their nana and pop because I have plans of my own later."

Now I know Joe is a snitch. He called Grayson when he disappeared on me.

"I'm glad to hear that, man. You deserve to be happy again, and my girls deserve to see their dad in love. They need to see how a man should love a woman so they'll never settle for less." His daughters are like my own kids, and I want the best for them the same as I do for my best friend.

"If you and Liv would move past your hang-ups and just talk to each other, your girls would have two male role models in their lives. If anything ever happened to me, I'd expect you to step in and be their father. Fix the issues in your marriage, Ryder. It's time to take your head out of your ass and realize what you have right in front of you. She could be snatched away without notice, and there won't be a damn thing you can do about it then." He takes a long drink of his beer, knowing I can't argue with him after what he went through when he lost his wife.

"Isn't it time for you to go get ready for your date?" With my forearms resting on the bar, I glare at him—until he laughs in my face. What are best friends for, right?

"Yes, it is. Let me give you a ride home first though. I'm not sure I trust leaving you here alone. Cyndi just walked in and she's watching you like a hawk, ready to swoop in and snatch up her prey. She's waiting for me to leave." He finishes his drink, drops a couple of bills on the bar and stands.

"Go. Don't worry about me. She isn't even a temptation. I won't drive since I walked here, anyway. Have fun tonight." I wave him off when he hesitates to leave, and he reluctantly walks away.

After I settle my tab, I begin my trek back to my quiet and lonely condo. I've never told anyone what I shared with Grayson. Maybe if I'd told Liv, she and I would be in a very different place today. My confession could've encouraged her to share more with me. Having my full support behind her artistic ability certainly would've changed our course.

But admitting my shortcomings as a man has been harder than I can express.

When I reach my building, I can't make myself go inside. It's summer in Montana, and we don't get a lot of warm nights here. Instead, I keep walking and cross the old wooden bridge, heading out of town. Then I turn right, behind the Mason Creek welcome sign, and walk along the shore of the lake. Memories rush back to me of all the good times we've had here on this water, hitting me like a tsunami.

The town lights twinkle in the darkness. The surrounding area is rural, so there aren't many distractions from the atmosphere the town has worked hard to maintain. Everyone knows most everyone else around here, and they gossip like a bunch of busy bees working, but these same people would help you out of a jam in a heartbeat. The sense of community here is strong.

I don't recall feeling that sheltered and protected sense when we were off at college. Also, I can't imagine Grayson raising those precious little girls anywhere else. My wanting to leave here comes down to two undeniable reasons—my pride and my privacy. Everyone I know being privy to my medical problem isn't something I can live with, and it'll get out sooner or later. Having to look my customers in the eye afterward would send me right over the edge. I'd know exactly what their whispers were about.

Is there another way around this conundrum? Everyone in our circle knows how much Liv wants children. Grayson mentioned other ways of getting that done, but I've already looked into it. Besides the cost, there's no guarantee in vitro fertilization will even work. Months of disappointment will only add to the stress we're already under.

The light wind causes small ripples on the water, pulling me under the mesmerizing effect. The reflection of the twinkling lights dances on the waves, lulling me into a contentment I haven't felt in a long time. I find a good place to sit on the bank, be alone with my thoughts, and figure out my next move. My head says I should listen to Grayson and just have a talk with Liv. We both need to lay all our cards on the table and see what kind of hand we've been dealt before it's too late.

LIV WASN'T KIDDING WHEN SHE SAID SHE'D BEEN busy planning the 'Draw the Shades' fashion show. When I walked into Java Jitters for my morning cup of high-octane fuel, the fliers were everywhere. Over the last few weeks, I've kept my head down and focused on my business. I've been going in early and leaving late, minimizing the time I spend alone in my condo.

I've also skipped the last four marriage counseling sessions in favor of doing anything that didn't involve facing Liv yet. One look at me, and she'll be able to read my mind because I can't think of anything else. She'll know something else drives my reaction, and there'll be no getting out of talking about it then. I'm just not ready yet. I'm not in the right frame of mind to be rational about it.

"Hey, Ryder." Jessie steps up to the register as I walk in. "You want the usual today?"

"Yeah. No need to change a good thing, right?" I quip.

"Oh, I don't know about that. Variety is the spice of life, they say. Maybe you need some new coffee spice to perk you up." She smiles genuinely, so I know there's no hidden jab in her words. Promoting her products only makes her a good business owner.

"You're right. Surprise me with whatever you want me to have today. Let's spice things up a little." I chuckle at the thought of a new coffee changing my life.

"Are you going to Liv's 'Draw the Shades' event this weekend? Sounds like it'll be a lot of fun." She passes the cup across the counter to me as I hand her the cash.

"I don't think she has anything that'll fit me." Not only did I not know about it until today, but that's not quite my scene, anyway.

"You haven't heard then? She added some men's pieces to her collection. A few of our local legends will model her new designs. She's sure to have a packed house. Everyone has been talking about it for days." Jessie nods toward the cup in my hand. "What do you think?"

I've been listening intently to the conversation

about Liv including male models in her show, so I haven't even tried the new concoction yet. One sip, and I'm hooked. "This is delicious. What is it?"

"Cinnamon dolce. It's been around for years. You really should get out more often, Ryder." She laughs good-naturedly.

"Pick out something new for tomorrow morning. Surprise me." I hold up my cup in a cheers gesture as I leave.

Before I reach the jewelry store, my phone vibrates with a text. When I look at the screen, I'm surprised to see Liv's name.

We have a meeting with Judge Nelson today at 10 am at the courthouse.

WITH ONLY TEN MINUTES TO SPARE, I CHANGE course and hurry to make it on time. I step into the courtroom just before the judge makes his entrance. When we're all seated, he calls Allie up to question her.

"Did you meet with Ryder and Liv King, as directed?" He looks at me when he asks her the question.

"Olivia King attended as mandated, but Ryder missed several sessions." After Allie tells on me, I refuse to meet the judge's glare.

"Were you able to make a determination in the allotted time?" His normally gruff voice takes on a new depth of bass.

"Yes, your honor, I've made a determination. In our sessions, I witnessed several passionate arguments regarding issues in their marriage. At other times, they agreed on vital topics and even seemed excited to be with each other. My interaction with them revealed they share a deep love for each other, rooted in an ongoing connection that's not easily broken.

"This insight tells me they both still care very deeply. Couples who are truly ready for a divorce and who no longer love each other don't care enough to fight. They're more willing to avoid any confrontation simply to remove themselves from the equation. It is my professional opinion that Mr. and Mrs. King remain deeply in love with each other, despite their significantly stubborn personalities."

"Thank you, Allie. I'm inclined to agree with you, especially if the rumors around town are true. At any rate, they haven't satisfied the court's requirement for waiving the six-month separation. The count resets as of today. Perhaps you two can work out the custody arrangement within your extended time."

The slamming of his gavel was probably unnecessary, but it made his point quite eloquently. As we turn to leave, Liv whisks a tear away from her eye, ducks her head, and quickly leaves the room.

I may have pushed her away a little too hard this time.

CHAPTER 15

Olivia

"Annie, my phone is possessed or something. It keeps giving me sales notifications on the same item." My phone vibrates again. "Maybe I need to restart it."

"There's nothing wrong with your phone, Liv. Since *Entranced* made their giveaway announcement, we can't keep up with the demand. Jasmine and I have already contacted the manufacturer, but you may want to give them a call to follow up. I think they'll need to plan some overtime soon." The chime over the door rings when a customer walks in, drawing Annie's attention. "But don't think this gets you out of telling us what happened in court last time you went. You've been very closed-mouthed about it."

Court. Don't remind me.

Ryder walked out on me after Tate's last column spilled my biggest secret. Hearing Allie say we're still deeply in love and connected to each other hurt more than I ever knew possible. We're obviously not since our last joint session ended in disaster and he hasn't been back since.

Going to marriage counseling alone is humiliating.

Before starting the sessions, we gave him an extra few minutes each time to join us. But he never showed, so Allie and I focused on me and why I hid my sketch business from everyone. She helped me understand it was a defense mechanism. If no one knew I created the clothing pieces, they couldn't use the accomplishment that made me proudest to hurt me. Keeping it from Ryder wasn't intentional. I simply found it easier to keep it from everyone or no one at all.

Had he shared in my excitement, he would've wanted to share it with others. If he'd been embarrassed by me, he would've crushed me and my livelihood.

I had no way out—until I was outed by the magazine. Then it became a chance of a lifetime I couldn't turn down. The magazine surprised me with the announcement of their giveaway before the feature article has been released. My best guess is that marketing ploy helps them sell more copies of the upcoming issue as much as it's helped increase my sales. But giving me advance notice of their plans would've been nice.

Annie's right about contacting the manufacturer though. At the rate the orders are coming in, we'll be buried under merchandise invoices before much longer. After speaking with my contact and explaining the entire situation, I think we have everything worked out to meet the new demand.

This is simultaneously the most exciting, stressful, happy, and sad time of my life. I need girl time with my bestie, but I can't afford to step away from the madness right now. As if she sensed my turmoil, my phone lights up with her name.

"Did my Faith radar go off?" I answer with a chuckle.

"It sure did. I heard you call for me all the way over here. How are you doing, sweetie?" I can hear the concern in her voice. There's no use in trying to hide anything from her.

"I'm overwhelmed, if you want the truth. This should be the best time of my life, but my heart isn't fully in it." I drop my head in my hand, then Kiwi lights on my shoulder. "At least Kiwi still loves me. She's been especially affectionate this week."

"Has she said any other crazy phrases?"

"No. But I figured out where she was getting them.

I caught Hattie teaching her naughty words and giving Kiwi treats for saying them. I've had to ban Hattie from the back doors to both my and Ryder's stores. We leave the doors open and only use the screens when she's in her cage, and Hattie was making good use of that time."

"That woman is always up to something Have you talked to Ryder since the big blowup?"

"No, not a word. Even when we swap Kiwi for our week with her, he sends someone else in his place." Now is as good a time as any to fill her in on my new six-month waiting period before our divorce is final—and what Allie said about our relationship.

"Ouch. I'm so sorry, honey. What can I do to help?" The pain in her voice for me nearly does me in, but I've done well with not breaking down so far and I'm not about to start now.

"All I can do is take it one day at a time. I don't know of anything else to do. Drinking doesn't help. I've tried." I laugh, but it's true. Nothing helps.

"We need our own therapy session. I'm fairly certain you're still in denial and need a come-to-Faith meeting. I'm coming over tonight and Hope will be with me." She doesn't leave any room to argue the point, and I love her for it.

"You know where to find me. You and my baby girl are always welcome to come over anytime you want."

We disconnect after setting our plans in stone, and

I resume handling all the preparations for my upcoming event. When I look up again, the first thought that enters my mind is, who did I piss off in a previous life to deserve this today?

"Hello, Olivia. We're sorry to bother you at work, but we don't want to waste another minute if we can help it." His eyes plead with me.

"Mom. Dad."

What the hell do they want? Did I just say that out loud?

"What can I do for you?"

Mom hesitates to speak and looks around nervously, so I escort them to my office in the back.

"Your father and I want to apologize for what happened when you came to visit last month. We were caught off guard by the articles at first, but then by your questions and accusations. Now that we've had time to think about it and reflect on everything, we realize how badly we handled that conversation. We love you so much, and we're insanely proud of you. We've never regretted having you, sweetheart, but I understand our actions didn't always show that. We're so sorry, and we want to fix what we've done wrong. We didn't know how to be parents, and you suffered because of our inadequacies."

They literally could knock me over with a feather. They're the last people I expected to see in my store.

My parents are here, apologizing for years of passive neglect and asking for another chance to make it right.

"We had a long talk with Jeannine about our shortcomings and how it affected you over the years. We're obviously late in recognizing where we failed you. But Olivia, you were never a mistake. We have never regretted one minute of having you as a daughter. Give your old man a chance to make up for a lifetime of regret, precious."

Precious... a long-forgotten memory tickles the back of my mind. Daddy used to call me that when I was a small child. Holding me in his arms. Picking me up and carrying me around the backyard with him. Where have these memories been?

"Of course." I shrug my shoulders and bite the inside of my cheek to stall the emotions building inside. "You're my parents. What child doesn't want to be loved by their mom and dad?"

"You were always so fiercely independent and didn't want any help with anything. We didn't think you much wanted us around. We tried to give you enough space to be your own person, but we never meant to make you feel alone or abandoned." The tears streaming down Mom's face reveal more to me than her words. I've only seen her cry once in my life, and that was when her mother died.

"I'm still stubborn and independent, but I'm

willing to bend on occasion." They encircle me in a group hug, and I feel the walls I've built around my heart start to crack a little more. My emotions have been getting the best of me lately.

"We're staying in town now instead of traveling so much. We'd love to have you over for dinner. Every night if you'd like." Mom's awkwardness is endearing. At least she's trying, and I'm grateful for that.

"Dinner sounds great. I haven't had a decent home-cooked meal in so long. Jeannine spoiled us with her cooking because nothing else measures up now. Maybe you'd like to come to my lingerie show. The number of RSVPs I've received back is incredible. It'll be a big night." I'm not sure how they'll react to it, but I'm extending the olive branch, anyway.

"That sounds amazing. You'll have to tell me all about it. I'm afraid I'm a little out of the loop when it comes to local events."

I grab one of the fliers and hand it to her, then I explain the premise of it, including that it was mostly Ryder's idea. Then I go on to explain what *Entranced* is doing to help my business, and how much of an impact it's already having on my sales.

"I still can't believe you designed these pieces all along." My dad looks both surprised and impressed. "You are a talented young lady. I wish you'd confided in me years ago. We have so many friends in the business world who would've loved to invest in this endeavor."

"Thanks for the vote of confidence, but I wanted to do this on my own. Riding someone else's coattails isn't exactly my style." I smile, showing my gratitude, but there's a certain pride that comes with earning the recognition on my own.

"We won't keep you any longer, then. You're welcome home any time you want to come over, and I will definitely be here for your big event. I wouldn't miss it for the world." Mom kisses my cheek as she hugs me again, then Dad joins in.

Our relationship may feel strange for a while as we test the waters of our new normal, but I believe we'll find our way. It's incredible what a heartfelt apology can accomplish. Had they not initiated this reconciliation by showing up in my shop unannounced, we wouldn't have the opportunity to correct our past mistakes and move forward together. My stubbornness wouldn't have allowed me to be the one to bend first.

Thoughts of Ryder slip into my mind like a thief in the night. Comparisons of my relationship with my parents and with Ryder bombard me. Ryder and I are both obstinate, but he always forgave quicker and was ready to move forward before I was. My problem was I liked to hold on to grudges a little longer. Did my need for independence and autonomy drive an invisible wedge between us until I completely pushed him away?

One more thing to talk to Allie about. Add it to the growing list.

When I emerge from the back room, Annie and Jasmine are closing out the till for the night. The store will be closed for the next few days while we rearrange the floor, have the stage built, and draw the shades for the big reveal of my new line.

I'm so excited I may vomit.

***

"Tonight's the night." I turn to Faith for support for the fifteenth time today. "I'm going to throw up."

"No, you're not. You're going to make this town go up in flames with your sense of style." She shakes her head at me, then slings her arm around my shoulders and hugs me to her. "I'm so proud of you, sweetie. This place looks amazing."

Faith and her employees are working during the show tonight, helping the models become stage-ready with their hair and makeup. She's also my emotional-support human and the only reason I'm halfway sane right now. "Putting this event together has drained every bit of energy I have. My plan is to sleep a solid week when this is over."

"Listen, you've transformed this store into an elegant art gallery. The pink and white flowers perfectly match the shade of the runway. The lighting is amazing, and your models are all gorgeous. This will be an incredible success all the way around. Stop stressing. It's not good for your skin."

Faith knows how to calm me when I'm on the edge of a nervous breakdown better than anyone else I know.

Annie and Jasmine find me in the back checking last-minute preparations to tell me our guests are beginning to arrive. The shades on the front of the store are drawn, keeping the interior of the store a secret, and advertising the event at the same time. When I peek outside, I'm surprised to see the long line of people waiting to get in.

"Here we go." I unlock the door and welcome each person, then Annie and Jasmine direct them to the seating areas.

When the rows are all filled and the door is closed once again, I scan over all the smiling faces as I make my way to the stage. One person who's obviously missing is Ryder. I'd secretly hoped he'd be here to support me during this big night, but I guess he's beyond mad and simply over us. I step up on the runway and ask for everyone's attention.

"Thank you for coming tonight. I guess the cat's out of the bag now. Surprise! I'm the designer behind the Roots & Wings collection. You'll be the first to see all my new designs tonight. I'm thrilled to announce you'll also be the first to see my all-new line... of *men's* unmentionables." The crowd laughs, and a few people whistle with loud catcalls in their excitement. "Now I'll turn the runway over to the people you actually came here to see—the models!"

The main lights dim, and the spotlights take over, drawing everyone's full attention to each model as she makes an entrance. The room fills with *oohs* and *ahs*, making the butterflies in my stomach multiply. The ladies rush around backstage to change into the next outfit, then strut down the catwalk once again.

If I wasn't watching every detail of this event, I'd still know the very second the guys stepped out from behind the curtain.

Cole Jackson, our resident cocky, arrogant, and flirty playboy, is up first. Cole is always on a mission to make others smile. He takes to the runway like a fish takes to water. He's wearing the silky blue boxers with red stripes and white stars. One of the stars ended up in a rather strategic position on the fabric, and he makes sure to point out that specific spot as he walks.

When he reaches the end of the stage, the music immediately changes, and he starts doing his best *Magic Mike* impersonation. The crowd goes wild, and women all over the room jump to their feet. I suddenly wish I'd given out a pair of panties to each person so they could throw them onstage at him. I turn to Annie and Jasmine, and I can only imagine my face resembles a cartoon character. My eyes are bugged out of my head, and my bottom jaw is lying on the floor.

"Where did that music come from?"

"Cole." Their joint reply is all that needs to be said. The man is a walking spectacle, but give him a stage and an audience, he becomes a superstar on steroids.

Not to be outdone by his cousin Cole, Levi Jackson struts out next, wearing black and red Valentine-themed silky boxers and a matching smoking jacket. He jerks the jacket open wide, standing with his feet planted and looking a lot like a flasher. Then he quickly closes it and turns to face the other side of the room. His coy expression doesn't fool anyone. He's simply waiting for the perfect timing of the song. He throws it open again and joins Cole in the stripper dance.

In their quest to be number one, Cole and Levi start a friendly shoving match—pushing the other behind him to take over the full spotlight, that is. Tears of laughter stream down my face as I watch those two goofballs ham it up for the audience. People are up on their feet, waving dollar bills in the air, laughing with their friends, and thoroughly enjoying themselves. I haven't laughed this hard in forever, and it feels so good.

Then Will Murphy steps on stage. He may be a little wild, but he's a good-hearted kid. He's in all black silky boxers, but he's added more to his outfit than I originally slated... in the form of a beautiful lady on his arm. She's wearing one of my split-thigh night dresses in matching black silk. The music changes on cue with their appearance, and they begin a sexy salsa dance. The crowd cheers louder, making Cole and Levi stop their show and watch Will and his friend for a minute.

The two men lock gazes for a moment and shrug, then start salsa dancing too—with each other. My entire show has gone off the rails, but in the best way possible. The men and women in the audience are having a great time, the models have all converged on the stage together, and they're all switching dance partners like they're at a square dance.

While I'm wiping away tears again, I don't see the ambush approaching me on both sides. Cole is on my left, and Levi is on my right. They grab my arms and carry me out to what's now the most scantily clad dance floor Mason Creek has ever had. I'm sandwiched between two handsome men wearing nothing but their loose, silky underwear. They're both grinding against me—all in good fun—but this scene could easily be taken out of context. With my history of rampant rumors, I'd rather not stoke the fires if I can help it.

But this is my party, and I'll salsa if I want to. Besides, I can't easily extricate myself from their arms. Or legs. Or torsos. When the song plays out, I excuse myself and end our night of frivolity on a high note.

"I hope everyone enjoyed the show." Before I can finish my prepared speech, the room breaks out into clapping and cheers. "Even though I didn't arrange or even know about the male stripper show Cole, Levi, and Will performed for us, I want to thank them for being such good sports up here tonight. There's not a lot of demand for men's designer underwear in this small corner of the world, but they made it look like a household staple. To the female models, thank you all so much for making my lingerie look so good. To everyone who turned out tonight, thank you so much for spending your evening with us. If you're interested in any of the new pieces, we're now taking orders in the store and online. Good night, everyone."

When the last person finally leaves the store, I collapse on the stage from sheer exhaustion. After moving all the clothing and racks out of the building to set up the show, I'm already tired from just thinking about resetting the store to normal again. But that's a problem and a concern to start thinking about tomorrow. Tonight, I'm going to enjoy the afterglow of this major feat.

Faith drops down on the platform beside me and lies on her back. "What an awesome night. I'm so incredibly proud of you and all you've accomplished. You are going places, my friend."

CHAPTER 16

Ryder

For the past week, I've purposely avoided anything remotely related to Liv and her marketing festivities. I've skipped my morning coffee run, making it at home instead. Lunch has been reheated leftovers from the night before. The lonely, quiet night before. My internet surfing didn't include anything local since I know all the gossip is shared so freely.

I want no part of it. The less I know, the better.

"Son of a bitch." When I open my browser to the national news page, there's a viral video of Liv onstage with Cole and Levi Jackson. They're grinding all over her while she laughs and lives it up with them. Cole is one of the biggest playboys around, but his constant flirting is mostly harmless. My rational self knows this because I know him so well. Same for Levi, for the most part.

It's the irrational monster inside I'm dealing with now. The green one who doesn't want to see another man anywhere near touching my wife, much less dry humping her on stage while wearing almost nothing. If I allow my mind to examine the facts, I know neither guy is Liv's type, and she's too smart to fall for a smooth talker with a witty line. But that's a fleeting thought when I keep hitting replay on the video.

After waiting another week before engaging with anyone more than absolutely necessary, I realize I can't avoid the town forever. I decide to face the music and grab my standing order from Java Jitters on my way to work. When I walk in, Cole Jackson himself is in the middle of the store, recreating his moves with someone else. The morning crowd cheers him on with their laughter.

"And that, ladies, is how I became an overnight sensation. Once Tate posted that video on her blog, the rest was history. Instant. Viral. Video. There's my fifteen minutes of fame, immortalized on every social media site and news outlet." Cole beams with pride as he sips his coffee.

"I think you mean you were riding Liv's coattails

for her fifteen minutes of fame, don't you?" Jessie chuckles from behind the counter.

"Nope, not at all. Did you watch the video, Jess? I'm the one with all the moves and the dancing expertise. I have mad love and respect for Liv, but she clearly just stood there. All the talent is right here in my hips." He starts gyrating again like he was doing when I walked in. He looks up for the first time and notices me watching. "Ryder, my man. Tell them. Liv is great, but the woman can't dance. She has zero rhythm."

"Don't drag Ryder into your delusions, Cole. Liv is the one in New York City right now at *Entranced* magazine. She has more than fifteen minutes of fame in her future." Jessie turns her attention to me. "You want the usual or do you want a little spice today?"

"Spice me up, Jessie." I step to the register to pay. "Did you say Liv is in New York now?"

"Yeah. She's been up there a little over a week now. The day after the big event, the video of her designs went viral. The magazine extended their gala to ride the wave of free publicity. The article will still come out as planned, but they flew Liv up there to do an encore of her show on a much larger scale. Tonight is her big night in the spotlight. She was terrified, but we told her she couldn't pass up this opportunity. It's a once in a lifetime deal." Jessie finished making my cup of whatever the hell this is, and I walk out, more confused than I was when I walked in.

I had no clue all this was happening ten minutes ago. Now, I'm even more lost as to what's happening, or what I'm supposed to do about it. For someone who didn't want to travel or even leave Mason Creek, my wife is certainly going places. She's going with or without me. Seeing her in that video with Cole woke me up in ways I didn't even realize I was asleep.

I've never been the jealous type. Possessive, maybe, but every man is to a degree. But jealousy that ate me alive and kept me up at night was foreign to me until recent visions of my wife in the arms or bed of another man, sharing the intimate moments we've had together, torments me relentlessly. As does her secret life. If she kept her designs from me for so long, what else has she hidden away?

How can I even trust her again?

Before I realize it, I'm already approaching the store. My mind has been on everything except where I was, so I don't even remember the walk from the coffee shop. As I reach for the door, my phone vibrates in my pocket. I'm surprised to see Mom's number on the screen when I fish it out.

"Hey, Mom. Where are you and Dad today?" I walk through the store and head toward my office in the back.

"We're actually back in Mason Creek. We have a meeting with Grady today to discuss either buying or building a house here."

I'm stunned speechless.

"Uh, well, that's great, I guess."

"What kind of homecoming greeting is that?" Mom chuckles, but she's trying to hide the hurt behind her laughter.

"No, I didn't mean it like that. I'm sorry. You know I'm glad you're back. But the last time you talked about living here, you were adamant you hated the small-town, uncultured atmosphere. You felt smothered and cut off from the rest of the world. What changed your mind?" I'm genuinely curious because this was the last call I expected to get today.

"The world changed our minds. We've had wonderful adventures and experienced things we'd never seen in Montana, but we miss our son and our friends. We can vacation anywhere, but only one place has ever felt like home. It really is where our heart is and where we want to spend our golden years, surrounded by those we love."

"Wow. To tell you the truth, I'd pretty much given up on you moving back here. I was actually thinking about how I could move away and get out of this place too." I lean back in my chair and wait for her words of wisdom to guide me.

"Son, I'm afraid I put that thought in your head, and I'm sorry I did. I've lived in Mason Creek my entire life and thought I was missing out on everything the world had to offer. But our great country—and this great big world of ours—is made up of countless small towns just like it. We've been to so many places now, but all our favorites have been the small, intimate, out-of-the-way towns where we got to talk to the locals. You don't find the same hospitality and warmth in the big cities, son. Vacation wherever you want but make your home somewhere you'd feel safe raising your children."

There's that knife in my chest again, though she has no idea. I'd rather die a thousand deaths by horse fly bites than talk about that topic. With my mom or anyone else in this town. I'm even regretting sharing it with Grayson somewhat.

"Well, since Liv and I are separated, and she's off in New York City living her best secret life, that's not something any of us have to worry about. You'll say I'm still young and I'll change my mind. But I assure you, another trip down the aisle isn't anywhere in my future, so neither are kids." Besides traveling the world, the only other request my mother has made is to have grandkids one day. Seems I'm disappointing everyone and crushing the dreams of both the ladies in my life.

"About that... you know I love you more than life itself..."

"But." Here comes the other shoe.

"You're wrong in this case, sweetheart. You're taking her designs way too personally and reacting far too harshly."

"Too personally? How is this anything but personal?"

"What I mean is she didn't keep her designs from you specifically. She held that part of her close to her heart for years. I know it hurts she didn't trust you with that piece of her, but there's a reason why she didn't feel as though she could. What was that reason, Ryder?" Mom pushes even though she already knows the answer.

"Look, I already know I made her think I was ashamed of her business, and I feel like shit because of it."

How many people saw that in me and never said anything until now?

"You need to look deeper than that, Ryder. What you said is true, but you are her husband. That makes you her soul mate, protector, best friend, and confidante all rolled up into one person. If she didn't have you in her corner, she didn't have anyone. You can't blame her for doing something harmless, and what she loves, that helped support you both. When you go to her, think about that, son. That's how you'll win her back."

We talk for a while longer, mostly about their house plans and other business ideas they've picked up on their excursions. My thoughts keep returning to what she said about everything that Liv needed me to be. Can one person really fulfill all those needs? Then I think back on all the ways Liv supported and encouraged me over the years, and I realize how far off the mark I've been.

"New business ventures, huh? You're not interested in buying the store back from me?" I'm ready to sell. Today. I have no idea what I'll do instead because this is all I've ever known, but I'm ready to find out.

"We can talk about that if you'd like. Your dad and I didn't want to bombard you with too much all at once. But he has missed the sales part of the job. He loves talking to everyone and finding the perfect piece for them. There's no rush though. We've made some lucrative investments over the last few years, so we're better off than when we left town."

"Perfect. Once you're settled in again, we can make the deal happen and you'll be the proud owners of King Jewelry once again." This move will turn my life on its ear, but I'm ready for the change.

"Slow down, speedy. Let us get into a house first.

We haven't even been by to see you yet. How about we take you out to dinner tonight?"

"I'll never turn down a free meal with my parents. We can talk about your hostile takeover bid over some lasagna and salad."

"Sauce It Up Italian, it is. We'll meet you there at seven."

My day crawls by with Liv on my mind the entire time. When I close the store, Kiwi and I walk home. After I put her in the cage and make her supper, I jump in the shower and dress for dinner. My parents have been away for months on end, and I'm excited to see them again.

"Momma?" Kiwi tilts her head to the side, waiting for me to produce Liv on command.

"Momma's not here, sweet girl. She'll be back soon. I know you miss her."

"Daddy loves Momma?" She has made the statement before, but she's never posed it as a question.

"Yes, Daddy loves Momma. Daddy loves Kiwi too."

"Momma loves Kiwi?" The question gives me pause more than anything she's ever said. She's questioning her place in Liv's life, and I know without a doubt she feels our separation deeply.

"Yes, pretty girl. Momma loves Kiwi very much. She'll be home soon." Now I know exactly what Liv was trying to tell me about how my actions would hurt Kiwi. I can't do that to her... and I can't do this to us.

I have to talk to Liv.

My parents walk toward me from the opposite end of the block. "Paula and Chris King, the epitome of love after forty years of marriage."

"Look how handsome our boy is, Chris. We've been gone too long." Mom rushes to me with her arms open wide and a smile splitting her face in two.

Dad joins her in a group hug in the middle of the sidewalk right in front of everyone. "Hello, Ryder. We've missed you so much."

We move inside and are shown to our table. After we order, Mom stops talking in mid-sentence. "Look at Liv on the national news. She looks as beautiful as ever. But she does look a little green around the gills. She must be nervous."

I can't tear my eyes off the screen. Liv looks absolutely stunning in the formal gown she's wearing. Her hair is styled in an updo, exposing the delicate skin of her neck. Her makeup is much heavier than she usually wears it, but I have no doubt that's because of the cameras. The magazine's main gala is tonight, and Liv is one of their guests of honor.

"You're right. She seems very nervous. All those cameras and eyes on her are taking their toll. She's up there all alone. I don't know how she's doing it." She shouldn't be alone, but that's one fact I verified at work today. The viral video and the magazine exposure combined made her an overnight sensation. The internet is full of articles about her now. She's no longer only being covered by our local gossip girl.

"She's strong. Always has been. But even strong women need a safe haven to come home to, a shelter where they're protected from the storms life throws at us." Mom cuts her eyes over at me.

"She wouldn't trust anyone else to give her that." I know her too well, even if she had secrets she kept from me.

"Sounds to me like you have the perfect excuse to take the red-eye to New York." Dad sips his wine and raises his eyebrows at me. "You'll miss the main event, but there are other activities she's slated to attend. Pack your tuxedo and your best suits. You'll need them. We've got the store while you're away."

I'm on my phone reserving my seat on the next flight before he finishes his speech. Perfect excuse or not, she's mine, for better or worse, and I'm hers until death parts us. Probably even long after I'm gone.

"Kiwi already feels the pain of Liv being away. Can you two stay at my condo with her until I get back? I don't want her to think I've abandoned her too."

"You got it. We'll spoil our only grandchild until

you get back." Dad winks in jest, but he secretly loves Kiwi almost as much as I do.

We finish dinner, then I pack and make a few phone calls while they dote on Kiwi. I remind them of all the dos and don'ts with her before I leave, but I'm not sure they're even listening. When I finally rush out to the airport, the only concern on my mind is getting to my Livvy and being the pillar of stone she needs this week.

This King will do whatever it takes to protect and serve his queen.

CHAPTER 17

Olivia

When I left Montana for New York, I barely had time to pack much less alert everyone of my sudden departure. Annie and Jasmine are already on a group text with me, so I managed to get the store covered and asked them to pass the word. I'm sure the whole town knows where I am by now.

The cameras were all over the gala last night. I've never been so self-conscious of every move I made or every facial expression I had. How famous people do this all the time is beyond me. If I had someone following me to snap a picture every time I pulled my panties out of my crack, I'd just become a hermit permanently.

Part of the reason why I've kept my label hidden is because I don't like being in the spotlight. I'm fine being the woman behind the curtains, working the levers and pulling the strings. Being out front and center was more uncomfortable than I imagined it would be. Last night was incredible, every last moment of it, and I wouldn't change one second of it because it's an experience I'll never get to live again. All the compliments and appreciation of my work made me want to outdo myself when I create the next new set. But for that, I want to be far away from everyone else where my creative juices can flow freely.

There is another extravagant event tonight coupled with a formal dinner *Entranced* is having catered for specific high-profile advertising agency contacts. Their mission to feature and promote businesses owned by women has successfully launched the careers of many others into the stratosphere. I'll be rubbing elbows with the best and brightest in the luxe fashion advertising world, and I have no idea what to say to them. The world of two-thousand-dollar shoes is as far from my everyday norm as I am from home tonight.

My phone rings, pulling me away from my window seat and out of my trance. "Hello?"

"Hi, Mrs. King. This is Sandy, Jacqueline's assistant. I'm calling to confirm your schedule for this evening. Our driver will pick you up at your hotel and drop you off at the Liberty Warehouse in Red Hook. Ms. Rafferty has arranged a private showing of all your work, including the new pieces from your men's collection, and will set the parameters for advertising proposals. The interested agencies will have questions about your direction and goals for the future so they can determine how to best represent your brand. You'll want to have the answers prepared and rehearsed ahead of time. Do you have any questions?"

"Sandy, I've never been involved in anything like this before. What if no one wants to pick me up as a client? I mean, if I'm sitting there alone and no one's interested, I'll be mortified." Seriously, this is way out of my comfort zone, and I feel completely out of my league here.

Sandy bursts into a loud guffaw before quickly composing herself again. "I don't think you quite understand how this works. That won't happen. They respect Jacqueline's opinion and her prediction of future trends too much to jeopardize their working relationship with her. If she believes in your talent, so will they. She wouldn't have arranged this event and invited them otherwise. Will there be anything else?"

She asks the question politely enough, but her tone leaves no room for further discussion. It is simply the professional in her that won't allow her to end the call so abruptly. I'm truly alone in this, and I've never felt more lost.

"No, that's all. Thank you, Sandy."

We disconnect after she reminds me of the pickup time. There's a knock at my hotel room door a second later, and I'm surprised to find a courier delivering my prescribed outfit for the evening. Seems they've taken care of everything and aren't leaving anything to chance since the hair stylist and makeup artist arrive next.

Great. It only took me thirty minutes to remove all the stage makeup from my face last night.

After everyone's finished making me into someone I'm not, I barely recognize myself when I step in front of the mirror. The woman staring back at me looks as if she belongs in the world of high fashion in her exquisite dress, expensive shoes, and name-brand purse. Her hair is perfect. There's not a single strand out of place. The fiercest nor'easter wind couldn't penetrate the makeup that looks as though it's straight out of a supermodel's photoshoot.

The driver calls on his approach to my hotel, so I make my way down to the lobby to meet him. He opens the back door of the Mercedes sedan and I slide into the opulent interior. He navigates the city streets with ease as I watch the blocks go by one after the other. Before I know it, and before I'm ready, we come to a stop, and he opens the door for my exit.

Standing there waiting for me, at Pier 41 in Brooklyn, is my knight in a black tuxedo.

He looks so handsome in his finest dress clothes. His hair is styled exactly the way I like it—short on the sides and spikey on the top, with that sexy, intentionally messy vibe. It's just long enough for me to run my fingers through it and grab a handful. He shaved his beard closer to his face, simulating three days of stubble and enhancing his strong jawline. His jacket is a perfect fit, accentuating his broad shoulders and trim waist.

"Ryder." I say his name on a released breath. I've missed him more than I realized until this very second. "What... what are you doing here?"

"What I should've done all along. I'm here to support my wife, protect her from everyone else in the world, and give her all my love. If she'll have me."

Despite his tempting outward appearance, what draws me to him over and over again is the invisible connection I feel on a deeply physical level every time we lock eyes. We've always had a special bond, but this act of devotion is beyond anything I would've expected of him.

"She will."

Relief fills his features. He turns and steps beside

me, extending his elbow for me to take his arm. I slide my hand through and wrap my fingers around his bicep. Part of me is thankful to have a plus one at my side so I'm not alone tonight. But that's not the main reason I'm thrilled to have Ryder with me. I trust him with my life and my heart, and I finally realized that when I thought I'd lost him forever.

He reaches over and gently turns my face toward his. "I'm sorry I made you feel anything but valued, appreciated, and respected. But I know where my place is now, and I'll never forget it."

"Where's that?" My reply is barely a whisper over this lump of emotion clogging my throat, but it's enough.

"Wherever you need me. Nowhere else."

"I need you beside me, anywhere I am." He has no idea how much I need him. Always have. Always will.

"You have me, come heaven or hell. Good times and bad. Blue jeans and cowboy boots or tuxedoes and dress shoes. I'm yours until the end of time."

"I love you more than anything, Ryder. Normally, I'd warn you about making me cry and messing up my mascara, but the fifteen coats on my eyelashes will last for years." We chuckle together, releasing some of the bottled-up tension.

"Since we're dressed all fancy and we're already

here, let's go inside to dazzle the elite ad agencies. We'll have them eating out of your hand in no time."

We begin our trek inside the waterfront warehouse that hosts some of the most elegant weddings and other significant events in the city. Our rented space here is incredible. A light stone accent wall complements the dark red brick of the warehouse. Round tables with immaculate linens, place settings, and centerpieces are perfectly arrayed to allow mingling. Short strings of lights hang from the ceiling, twinkling like a million stars in the sky. Large glass sliding doors are open fully, allowing the breeze from the water to permeate the room as guests enjoy the view from the expansive balcony.

"Ryder, let's sneak out the back door and call an Uber. I don't think I can do this." My hands are clammy, I'm starting to hyperventilate, and I'm sure I'll trip in these four-inch heels any second now.

"Not a chance, babe. This is your moment to grab this business by the balls and make it your bitch. Are you afraid of failing... or succeeding?"

"Yes." My answer is completely honest.

"Either way, I'm here to catch you or help you fly as high as you can soar. You're not in this alone anymore."

"They'll want to know what my future plans are

and what direction I'm taking my company. Ry, I don't know what to tell them."

"I have a couple of ideas if you're interested in hearing them." He raises his eyebrows as he waits for my stunned reply.

"Uh, yeah, of course I want to hear them." I can't believe he has more suggestions for my lingerie.

"One line can be more exclusive and higher-end than the others. Make pieces to include some rare gems in the final product so they'll sparkle more. My other idea is to create themes for your merchandise. You can do a wedding theme, honeymoon theme, holiday themes, costume themes, and make the men's and women's lines match. Start with those and see how they react." He takes two flutes of champagne from a passing tray and hands one to me.

"Those are genius ideas, Ryder. The exclusive line alone gives me so many design ideas, although they will be extravagantly expensive. But you're right, that caters to a different buyer demographic. The theme idea could cross lines too. I'm so excited to start working on the sketches for these new ideas."

"So my marketing degree wasn't a total waste of time, huh?" He winks then sips his champagne. "Are you going to drink that?"

"Not right now. My stomach is in knots. I'm also afraid I'll spill it on this twenty-thousand-dollar dress they gave me to wear or throw up when someone talks to me. Plus, holding the glass gives me something to do with my hands." I smile and shrug, accepting my inability to truly fit in with the crowd surrounding me.

His dazzling smile lights up his face. "I hope you never change. You're adorable and perfect exactly as you are. Come on, babe. Let's go razzle-dazzle all your guests together." He jerks his head to the side and takes my hand in his free one.

We make our rounds through the room, with Ryder doing most of the ice-breaking and introductions. Once the conversation starts flowing, I chime in and manage to add a few witty remarks and intelligent points regarding the topic at hand. If Ryder hadn't been standing there when I got out of the car, I probably would've already left by now. But he gently urges me to keep going with every new conversation we have.

Jacqueline Rafferty, the woman in charge of my fashion world, arrives with a flurry of activity and a rush of excited chatter. She takes the stage and steps in front of the microphone.

"Good evening and thank you for joining us tonight as we focus on another company founded and operated by a woman with high hopes and attainable goals. As you all know, *Entranced* magazine has a long history of supporting our fellow women in business ventures we believe in.

"It's my profound honor to endorse Olivia King, owner and founder of Roots & Wings lingerie. Not only does she have a keen eye for fashion, she has her finger on the pulse of what women of all ages need and want. Her vision is to make every woman feel sexy and desirable, erasing the constraints and doubts that have held so many back from what they really want.

"If you haven't met her and her handsome husband yet, I urge you to get in line as soon as possible. This young lady has an incredibly bright future ahead of her. Also, you're being treated to a private showing of her most recent creations for both women and men over tonight's dinner. Enjoy."

With my smile in place, I turn to Ryder and whisper without moving my lips. "She hasn't met you. How did she know you were here with me?"

"I made a few calls to people from college until I found someone who knew someone who knew her. It wasn't easy, but we got through to her and explained the situation. She loved the idea of me being here for you, so she added me to the guest list."

"You went through all that trouble to be here with me?" I can't hide my surprised expression.

"There's nothing I wouldn't do to be with you, Liv. There's nothing too hard for me to accomplish. There's nowhere that's too far for me to go. I've loved you my entire life, and I'll love you forevermore."

The ad agencies we haven't talked with yet begin making their way to our table, forming a line as Jacqueline instructed. During dinner, while others watch the show, we continue talking and engaging with people who can change our lives forever. Over the next two hours, Ryder and I answer questions until we're hoarse and have no energy left. Our cheeks hurt from smiling and our throats are as dry as the Sahara. A waitress stops to replace our table's water pitcher, and we greedily refill our glasses.

When the event is over and the hour is way past my bedtime, Ryder and I walk outside together and find the same car and driver waiting for us. Ryder hesitates for a moment, unsure of what I expect him to do. I clinch my fingers tighter around his hand.

"They gave me one hell of a suite at the hotel. The room is huge, and I'm the only one in it. Would you like to spend the night with your wife?"

"Only every night for the rest of my life."

We get in the car and stay close to each other. It's late for us, but we can't stop staring at the still full streets of the city that never sleeps. The night life here is incredible, but I don't think we can swing it after the evening we've had. In fact, I know I can't. Everything I've done lately has zapped my stamina with all the stress I've been under. We reach the hotel and head straight to the suite.

"Thank you for tonight. Without you, ten agencies wouldn't have promised a proposal within the week. This also wouldn't be both the most exciting and the scariest time of my life. But I'd much rather face it with you than without you, that's for sure." I wrap my arms around his waist, and he does the same to me.

"You did all the work. I only started a few conversations." He shrugs as if it's no big deal.

"No, my love. You did a lot more than that. Ry, I'm sorry I kept this from you and didn't let you be part of it too. I wasn't trying to shut you out. I just didn't want to face the possible rejection. But now I realize I didn't give you a chance when I assumed you'd be one of those who looked at me differently. That wasn't fair to you or me, and I regret every moment of not letting you be my partner." I cup my hands on his face, keeping our gazes locked in place.

"Thank you for saying that. I do appreciate the sentiment. But I've realized why you didn't include me, and it's my fault. Every time I made you feel ashamed for your talent or that I was embarrassed by your products, I pushed you farther into that corner. You never should've questioned how I'd react. That fault doesn't lie with you. Please forgive me for making you feel anything less than the queen you are." He lightly presses his lips to mine.

That's all it takes. One touch, and my body's on fire

for all of him. That small kiss becomes urgent and demanding as our teeth clash and our tongues swirl. Our hands roam until every shred of clothing is left in a pile on the floor. Losing myself in Ryder is so easy to do. He knows exactly which button to push and when to do it. The way he makes love to my entire body is pure art. I've never been left wanting more. He's never hurried to finish, putting his own pleasure before mine.

The bright lights of the city stream through the crack in the curtains, illuminating the dark room as we lie in the sweet afterglow of our reunion. He's on his back and my head is on his chest. The lub-dub rhythm of his heartbeat has always lulled me to sleep.

"Babe?" His voice is soft in the dark, but I feel so much tenderness in it.

"Hmm?" I don't move from my comfortable spot.

"Don't take this the wrong way. I have a question for you."

"Okay." I'm already taking it the wrong way. He regrets tonight. He's seen the craziness our life could become, and he wants out. So many doubts and questions invade my mind in the span of a split second.

"Is there anything else you haven't told me? I'm not accusing, and I won't be mad. Just tell me now if there's anything I should know." His fingers continue to stroke the skin along my spine... while I hesitate and gather my courage.

"There's one thing I haven't told you. It's a fairly recent development." I sigh deeply.

"Go on." He doesn't stop showing his love.

"I found out this morning... I'm pregnant."

His hand stills.

CHAPTER 18

Ryder

After a full minute of stunned and awkward silence, I'm finally able to formulate a complete thought to respond to the latest one hundred megaton bomb Liv just dropped on my head.

"What?"

Smooth, slick. Most articulate and thorough.

My question also came out a little harsher than I intended.

I'm simply in complete shock and unsure of how I'm supposed to feel about this. Every emotion known to man courses through my veins, heating my blood and raising my temperature. My heart just dropped twenty-one floors to the lobby, leaving me here to wrestle with the aftermath, and my head is spinning out of control.

Liv raises her head, and the first emotion I see in her expression is fear. Her reaction alone hurts. She has nothing to be afraid of when she's in my arms.

"Babe, I'm sorry. There's something I need to confess to you so that you'll understand. I haven't exactly been Mr. Forthcoming myself."

She sits up, pulling the sheet with her to cover herself, shielding her heart as she waits to hear what I have to say. "I'm listening."

I slide up until my back rests against the headboard and take her hand in mine to reestablish our connection. "First, I need you to breathe because it's not as horrible as the scenarios that are flying through your imagination right now. You'll be mad at me for keeping it from you, and you have every right to be. All I ask is you hear my full story before your kick me out of your suite naked."

A small smirk forms on her face. "Thanks for the great idea. Continue."

"Let me ease your mind by assuring you I'm thrilled you're pregnant. I can't wait to have a baby with the love of my life. My reaction wasn't out of anger, I promise."

Her bottom jaw drops to her chest. "But you never

wanted kids. You wanted to travel and see the world. A big family was never in the cards for you."

"That was the perfect excuse to hide the truth, Liv. We've been married a long time and have been together even longer. We've never really been careful to avoid a pregnancy. We've been more than a little lax with any type of protection. I think we both just assumed we'd deal with it when it happened because we knew we'd be together regardless of when we had to face that responsibility.

"But then I realized how much time had passed and we'd never had so much as a scare, and I started getting worried. So, I went to a specialist, who pretty much told me I'd never be able to get you pregnant. How could I tell you I'd never be able to give you the one thing you wanted so much? Now I realize it was my fear ruling me, but I was afraid I'd lose you to someone who could provide that big family you've dreamed about. On the other hand, I loved you too much to keep that dream from you. Obviously, I've never been able to refuse you since we've had sex after every mediation meeting."

When someone who rarely cries has large streams of tears flowing over her cheeks and can barely speak because of the sobs, it's more than disconcerting. It's downright scary.

She drops the sheet and climbs on my lap, straddling me and cupping my face in her hands. When she finally catches her breath, she stares deep into my eyes. "Ry, how could you not tell me what you were going through? That must have been pure hell on you, and you carried that burden all alone. I would've helped you. Did you think I'd stop loving you?"

"Liv, none of this is on you. I felt like less of a man, and because of that, I didn't tell anyone. I didn't want to see the pity when others looked at me, or hear the whispers about why we didn't have kids. I didn't want anyone to know I couldn't father children, but I certainly didn't want anyone blaming you for it. Getting out of town and away from everyone we knew seemed like the perfect solution. Our lives would seem like one big adventure and jumping from place to place would take our minds off anything else."

"What did the doctor say to you, exactly?"

"He said it would be highly unlikely I'd ever be able to impregnate you the old-fashioned way, and that we'd have to employ more creative methods if we wanted a family. At first, all I heard him say was I'm sterile. But I started doing more research and realized he meant in vitro fertilization and other scientific techniques of impregnating you. Still, the possible complications I read about with those procedures deterred me. I couldn't put you through failed implantations."

I'd blame myself for the repeated defeats if we had to go through multiple attempts.

"You are the most stubborn man I know, Ryder King. Of course I want a big family with you. You're my husband and I love you with all my heart. Having a baby with you felt like the next natural step in our relationship and thinking about you being a father was a natural aphrodisiac. But I fell in love with *you*, not your ability to give me children. I'm spending my life with you because you're my one and only love. If we weren't able to have a baby, my love for you wouldn't change. You confused me with your absolute refusal to even talk about it, and I began to think you hated our life together." The pain in her eyes spills over to her facial expression, conveying her torment more eloquently than her words ever could.

"If I could turn back time, I'd tell you what the doctor said that very day so we could figure it out together. I'm sorry I didn't give you the opportunity to be my partner and help make the decisions that impact both of us and our future. We're in this together, and I promise you this one thing. You'll know every single detail about my testicles from now on. You can examine them, up close and personal, any time you want." I wipe the last of her tears from her face and feel an intense sense of relief when she smiles again.

"Is there anything else, or was that all you had to

confess?" She arches one brow. "Now's your chance to get it all out in the open."

"That's all I've got, babe. You know everything else about me." I tuck a strand of her hair behind her ear.

"I'm glad to hear that. You just saved yourself from an embarrassing naked walk of shame through the hotel where everyone would have a chance to examine your testicles." She giggles maniacally as the visual floats through her mind. "Now that we know for sure it's possible, even if it's unlikely, I think we can both chill and take it one day at a time. All that matters is we're together. If we only have one baby, that's enough for me. We are connected, heart and soul, Ry. I'll stand by you, come what may."

"Liv, you're going to be a mommy." I intentionally lower my voice to keep her full attention on me.

Her eyes grow wide, and her jaw is slack. "Oh my gosh, Ryder. I am! With everything going on, it hasn't really hit me until just now. I mean, I knew this morning, but oh my gosh. What... how am I... will we... Ryder."

"Babe, you're rambling. Take a deep breath. I've got you." My smile is permanently attached to my face. My cheeks hurt from holding it in place for so long.

"So you're happy about this? I've been trying to figure out how to tell you all day. I wasn't sure how you'd take it since you were very convincing about not wanting any."

"I'm thrilled, babe. I'm going to be a father, and I get to spoil you for the next nine months."

She leans in to kiss me. "You get to spoil me for the rest of your life."

"Yes, obviously that's what I meant. The next nine months will only raise the bar." We laugh together, and for the first time in a while, I believe we'll be okay.

"Ryder, you're going to be a daddy." She uses my tactic against me. It works.

"Damn straight. I'm already looking forward to trying to get you pregnant again after this one is born." I waggle my brows suggestively.

"This is why I love you so much. You're always planning for our future."

After a long day and night, we settle back in the bed. Liv's back is against my front, my arm is draped protectively over her, and we lose the battle against exhaustion within minutes. When the bright morning sun wakes me, we're still in the same position as when we drifted off to sleep last night. Liv's still in a deep slumber, so I lie as still as I can to let her rest as long as she needs.

There were so many times over the past year I thought I'd lost her for good. Somehow, we've managed to hang on and pull through some of the hardest and darkest days we've ever had. But the trials and tribulations have made us stronger. The secrets and insecurities have made us both more aware of ourselves. Not that I had any valid reasons not to trust Liv before, but now I have no doubt she'll always stand beside me. There's no question in my mind that I'll do the same for her. Our time apart proved one fact—there's nothing we want more than each other.

Planning for our future, as Liv put it, has always come naturally to me. I've never seen my future without her in it. So my ideas and plans revolved around her and what we can do together. The jewelry store wasn't in my plans, but I'm grateful for the experience it's given me. That will help me execute my next idea, provided Liv's on board.

"What's on your mind, Ry?" Liv's sleepy voice breaks the silence.

"How'd you know I was lying here thinking about something?" She knows me far too well.

"Your body tenses up all over, and you scrub your fingers across your beard over and over. You always give yourself away when you're planning and scheming in bed." Her body shakes with laughter.

"Mom and Dad are moving back to Mason Creek. I guess living the hobo life isn't all it's cracked up to be. Anyway, I'm considering selling the store back to them and starting something new I think you'd enjoy being part of, and it's somewhat connected to your passion." After I count to three, I calm my Type A personality as I exhale, relaxing all my contracted muscles.

"That sounds truly intriguing. I'm ready to hear more." She rolls over to face me. "If we can do it together, you know I'm in."

"When you said you were helping your friend, Miranda, plan her wedding in Mason Creek, an idea took root in my mind. We could start a full-service wedding planning business. We know all the local contacts to arrange for the cake, flowers, catering, ministers, and rooms. We could carry the themes of your lingerie line into the wedding themes. Some of the packages would include your products. The jewelry store could also benefit from it through selling rings and small gifts for the bridal parties. We could market it as an all-inclusive service and have an à la carte menu."

"Where are we going to hold all these wonderful ceremonies?"

"Maybe we sell the house and the condo to buy a bigger place farther out of town. We can get a farm where we'd have a dedicated area for customers that's far enough away from the main house to keep it private. Eventually, we can add honeymoon cabins for the happy couples. If this takes off, I can go on and on with ideas to add to it. Christmas in Mason Creek may be cold, but it's beautiful. There are so many variations of Christmas-themed parties and ceremonies we can host." The more I talk about it, the more excited I become because this is something we can build together.

"You could custom design jewelry, Ry. You've always had a knack for that." She looks down at our hands. Our matching bands haven't left our fingers despite the direction we were headed. "But you definitely should handle the marketing for us. You have so many creative, outside-the-box ideas that could make all the difference. Do you enjoy marketing?"

"Yes, I really do. It keeps my mind sharp and makes me pay attention to trends."

"Maybe we should look into hiring a store manager for the day-to-day operations while you and I focus on the other priorities. I mean, I can draw the designs and submit them to the manufacturer from home. I'd be there with the baby and Kiwi most of the time. You can advertise and run the wedding business from the grounds. Plus, you'd be right there with us all the time." The hope and enthusiasm that were staples in her personality before our problems are back in full force. I finally feel as if I'm getting my Livvy back again.

"I love the way your brain works. Those are great ideas, and I completely agree. We need to write out our business plan then start getting the word out. Our little bundle of joy will be here before we know it. Once she's born, I won't want to let either of you out of my sight. I'm wrapped around your little finger. What can I say?"

"Do you think the whole town already knows I'm pregnant?" She smiles broadly.

"Not a chance. Let's not tell anyone until we can't hide your tummy anymore. We'll go to the doctor in another town so no one sees us and can start speculating. With all the new business you'll have when they pick the winning ad agency, you'll be too busy to hang around town anyway. We can be moved into our new place in no time. Grady can sell both places for us. What do you say?"

"Faith will kill me for keeping this pregnancy from her, but I will if you don't tell Grayson either." She holds her pinky out and I wrap mine around it.

"Deal. This is our happy, life-changing secret for as long as we're able to keep it from everyone."

On the flight back to Montana, Liv tells me about her 'Draw the Shades' night, and the shocking news of repairing relations with her parents. While I have a hard time believing they didn't realize any of the damage they caused her by their aloofness, I also realize I have to give them the benefit of the doubt. After all, there were vital secrets Liv and I kept from each other for various reasons. None of which were to harm the other, but the end result was the same. We didn't fully comprehend how our actions did hurt each other, though our love never waned. The consequence was a natural wedge driven between us, and we didn't know how to overcome that division for a while.

We've started on a new course now though, and we've learned from our mistakes. Some topics are painful and hard to breach, but we're committed to weathering all the storms life throws at us together. Neither of us is perfect. We've talked about always being merciful in those times when it becomes painfully obvious. Daily forgiveness will be our ongoing mantra. When we need time to work through a problem in our own head before sharing it, we'll give each other space. We're old enough to realize that will happen on occasion. We're not so naïve as to think life will be all rose petals and milk chocolates. Thorns and dark chocolate will always find their way in to muck things up.

"You know, I just thought of something." Liv leans toward me with a mischievous smile.

"This should be good. What is it?" One side of my mouth lifts on its own.

"Judge Nelson will never give us that divorce when he finds out I'm pregnant and you're the cause of it. He'll know what we've been doing."

"Everyone already knows what we've been doing. Grayson gave me hell for it after every time." I can't help but laugh because it's true. We couldn't stay apart even during our legal separation. "As for Judge Nelson, I think you're probably right That means you're stuck with me. Trapped like a fish in a net. Caught like a mouse in a trap. I have papers on you that say you're mine, and I'm not giving them up."

"Papers on me? I think you mean I have papers on you." She pokes my arm with a laugh.

"You certainly do. It would be inhumane to send me back to the pound now. You rescued me so you have to keep me."

"We need to call George first thing when we get back and tell him we've worked out the custody agreement. He'll be so happy. He'll probably take that vacation to Tahiti he keeps talking about. Do you think he'll send us a postcard?"

"George probably never wants to hear from us or contact us ever again."

When we finally arrive back in our little hometown, I see the old covered bridge in the distance and understand what Liv tried to explain to me before. We're home where we belong. Where everyone knows us and will be thrilled to see we're back together because they care about us. All we need is right here because we have each other.

CHAPTER 19

Olivia

We pull into the parking lot at Ryder's condo to pick up Kiwi and enough of his belongings for him to move back into our home until we have time to pack everything. He's ready to get Grady over here right now to list it for sale. I somehow convinced him to wait until tomorrow since we already have enough to do tonight.

Paula and Chris are snuggled on the couch watching television with Kiwi wedged between them when we walk in. This very scene is normal for Ryder and me on any given night, but seeing his parents treat our beloved bird as their grandchild makes me laugh. On the flight back from New York, Ryder talked about his parents moving back here with such affection, I knew he'd missed them more than even he realized. Having them here to help us throughout my pregnancy and after is a godsend.

They may have to teach my parents how to be grandparents.

"I see Kiwi has already taken control of the house and made sure she's well-cared for while we were away. You two didn't stand a chance, did you?" I approach them with my arms extended and hug them while they remain in their seats.

"She has bossed us around the entire time. She's spoiled rotten." Chris scratches her head as he speaks. The smile he's wearing belies his gruff tone.

"No argument here." Ryder wraps his arms around me from behind and rests his chin on my shoulder. "Kiwi definitely knows she's loved."

"It seems you two may have some news to share with us. I can't quite put my finger on it, but something is different." Paula puts her finger over her lips and playfully gives us the side-eye.

"We may have come to our senses and decided we're better off together. Not that we've managed to stay apart for any length of time anyway." When I lean my cheek against Ryder's, Kiwi flaps her wings and lands on my shoulder.

"Look at her work her way between you two. No one gets affection if she's not part of it." Paula laughs and shakes her head. "Well, since you're both home, I guess Chris and I can leave. We're so happy to have you back, Liv. We love you."

"I love you too, Mom, and I've missed you so much. Ryder said you and Dad are here to stay. Welcome home."

We hug and kiss goodbye with promises to make up for lost time in the coming days. Ryder packs a suitcase while I collect Kiwi's food and toys, then we continue on to our home. The awkwardness I was afraid would be between us is nowhere to be found. We easily move right back into our natural comfort zone with each other as we unpack his clothes and reset Kiwi's bird haven to its original glory.

When we finally relax on the couch, Kiwi nestled safely between us, everything feels right in my world at last.

"Momma. Daddy. Kiwi. Home."

"That's right, sweet girl. We're home—all of us, right where we belong." Ryder nuzzles her as he links our fingers together. "We're a family, and that's all that matters."

"Daddy. Treat."

"You're already had your treat for tonight." Ryder shakes his head from side to side. Kiwi bobs her head up and down.

It's a war of wills at this point. Who will win—the man or the bird?

"Daddy. Treat!" Her voice grows louder, and she spreads her wings.

"Fine. One more, but that's all." Ryder walks toward the kitchen as Kiwi ordered, and now we know who the boss around here is.

"You're going to be the meanest daddy ever. I can already see it now." He always gives in to Kiwi's demands. He doesn't stand a chance with our child.

"I will be a pillar of stone." He flexes his muscles to emphasize his strength.

"Your body may be, but your heart is as soft as a down pillow. This baby will own you and we both know it."

He pretends to be thoroughly offended for a moment before his smile breaks through. Then he shrugs his shoulders and lifts his hands with his palms up. "What can I say? There's no use in even trying to deny that. You've owned me since the day we met, and I wouldn't have it any other way."

He returns with chopped vegetables for Kiwi and movie theater buttered popcorn for us. We've barely gotten into our movie choice for the night when our phones ping with messages. We look at each other and roll our eyes at the same time.

"The news is out. Everyone knows we're back

together now. We probably won't even have to call George by morning. No one in town will be in the dark by then." Ryder takes a swig of his beer and turns off his phone without bothering to look.

I'm not that strong. Not after the last big surprise that knocked the wind out of my sails.

When I raise my phone, I'm not surprised to see messages from Faith, but the texts from Mom, Dad, Jeannine, Annie, and Jasmine are all out of the ordinary. In fact, I'm pretty sure I've just entered into the twilight zone. Something major has hit the airwaves. As I scroll through the messages, a common theme immediately forms.

"Ry... they're saying I'm on the national news channels again. Apparently, it's all about the magazine gala night and the next night with the ad agencies. *Entranced* magazine caused a frenzy over my lingerie collection, and now *celebrities* are talking about my work. Mom and Dad want to invest in my business to help me scale up. I'm a little overwhelmed right now."

"Breathe, babe, or you're going to pass out on me. We knew this exposure would bring major changes to your business. That was the whole point, right? You're no longer the boutique store on the corner. You're becoming a major brand. That's a good thing, love." Ryder strokes my cheek with his fingertips. "You'll go from small production orders to mass producing factories, but everything will be okay."

"You're way too calm about this. I feel like I need a paper bag to breathe into now." I fan myself with my hands. "Is it hot in here? I think the heat is on."

"The more your name is shared, the more businesses you'll hear from because they'll want a piece of the pie. I'm not worried about being inundated with orders. That's a wonderful problem to have. We'll face each step together though. But tonight, we're celebrating something special, and the world doesn't get to steal our time. We'll get back to work tomorrow after we pick up your car from the airport." He leans over to kiss me, effectively erasing all the concerns swirling in my mind.

"You're the best man I know, Ryder. I love you."

"I love you too, babe. Forever and ever."

THE LAST TWO WEEKS HAVE BEEN ONE CRAZY thrill ride after another. Social media influencers bought some of my products, riding on the coattails of the news clips, and gave them their own very thorough reviews of my work. This is exactly why I've hidden my identity behind a vague label name the entire time I've been in business. Most assessments were professional and supportive, but those handful who tore me apart with their harsh words were hard to take. I'm not allowed to defend myself or point out their obvious errors, so I've stopped reading reviews altogether.

It's for the best because I don't believe the glowing reviews and the negative ones hurt my creativity. I'll continue making what I like the way I like it. If others agree, I'm thrilled. If not, it's their prerogative to be wrong. Either way, I'll remain blissfully unaware. The emails I've received from the sweet women who gush over how my work has helped them are what sustain me. Sometimes they have great suggestions for additions or improvements that I can use to modify existing products or include in future projects.

Today, Mom and I are virtually touring a larger apparel manufacturing facility and talking to the executives about existing and future demands. My current contact is too overwhelmed to take on more orders. The larger scale and increase in projected volume also get us the bulk discount deals. This move may turn out to be even more lucrative than I ever anticipated. My initial panic morphed into excitement, and now that I've found my stride, I finally feel pride in being the woman behind the curtain.

I'm the brains and talent behind the scenes, and

finally I can say that without boasting or feeling conceited. I've nurtured and developed my skills, watched market trends and tried to get ahead of them, and researched and contacted production companies to be successful. The final jumping off point was agreeing to the magazine article that put me on the large-scale map. This business has been my baby from day one.

Speaking of baby, Ryder made an appointment with an obstetrician in Billings for our first prenatal visit. We still haven't told anyone here about the pregnancy. It feels so good—and sneaky—to keep this bundle of joy all to ourselves. I love the small-town atmosphere and the close ties we've made here, but the constant drama has always bothered me.

"Livvy, are you busy?" Ryder sticks his head in my office at home. "I wanted to run this by you, but I can come back later if I'm interrupting your creative flow."

"No, my love, come in. You never disturb me. You're pure inspiration for my designs." He plants a long, luscious kiss on me before pulling up a chair beside me.

"What do you think of this place? It's just outside of Mason Creek, heading toward Billings, but still close enough that we'd still be considered residents." He places the printed information about the house and fifty acres on my desk.

"It's gorgeous, Ry. I love the craftsman's design of

the house. Look at that gorgeous barn. There's plenty of space to make it the wedding venue. Can we put an offer on it before someone else gets it?"

"I'll call Grady and start the arrangements right now. Then I'm going to Mom and Dad's to talk about selling the store back to them. They settled on buying a house and Mom has already found the one she wants. She thinks having the business back will ensure Dad stays put. Do you need anything before I leave?" He moves the chair back and waits in the doorway for my answer.

"No, thank you for asking though. I'm calling Miranda to get more information about her upcoming nuptials and ask if she's interested in being our guinea pig for the full-service package. Then Mom and I have the video conference with the manufacturer. I have plenty to keep me busy today."

"All right. I'll bring dinner back from Wren's Café, so don't bother cooking." He disappears for a second then sticks his head back in. "Oh, and I've already fed Kiwi and gave her some snacks today, so don't let her fool you into feeding her again."

"Too late. I already fed her when you were in the shower, so she made you feel sorry for her and got extra food. We need to work out a system before she gets too fat to fit through the cage door."

He leaves on an exaggerated groan and an eye roll.

Typical day, but I wouldn't change it for anything. While I have a free minute, I locate Miranda's number and wait the couple of rings for her to answer.

"Hi, Miranda. How's my favorite bride-to-be?"

"Hi, Liv. I'm fine. How are you, famous lady? I'm surprised you're calling me, a lowly worker-bee from nowhere." Miranda's teasing tone and light chuckle at the end lets me know she's playing.

"You know, I almost had my assistant's assistant call you to say I didn't have time for you, but that felt a tad pretentious. I realized I need to stay connected to the little people, so I cleared my calendar just for you." We laugh together before I return the focus to business. "Are you eyeball deep in wedding planning?"

"Yes, I am, Liv, and I'm so overwhelmed and out of my depth, it's pathetic. All I wanted was to go to the courthouse and be done with it. But my fiancé won't have that for his bride. He wants the seven-course meal and swans gliding in the swimming pool while the full symphony orchestra plays the wedding march. I suppose this is other women's fantasy wedding, but it's not mine. It's causing me more stress than happiness."

I believe her. I can hear the stress in her voice, and it makes me cringe on her behalf.

"When is the big day? Have you set the date yet?"

"That's the other problem. We're already at the beginning of autumn. He wants a Christmas wedding... in Montana. We'll freeze our asses off." She sighs heavily into the phone. "I'm sorry to put all this whining and complaining on you. I'm just stressed and frustrated."

"Now I feel like an opportunistic asshole for saying this, but I can tell you need help. The reason I'm calling is because my husband and I are starting a new business here, and we wanted to offer you first dibs on being our guinea pig. We're starting a full-service wedding planning business. Ryder even has plans to turn one of the existing buildings into a chapel on some property we're looking at this week. What do you think?"

"I think hell yeah, Liv. You'd arrange the kind of ceremony I'd rather have anyway. Can I blame you when he asks why the angelic choir didn't descend from heaven to sing our praises?"

"You can absolutely blame me. I'm very well-versed in apologizing without ever taking full responsibility for someone else's ridiculous demands. If you want a Christmas wedding, we can push for an expedited construction to make sure everything is perfect for you. I'll call Ryder as soon as we hang up and tell him to get busy."

"You're so lucky, Liv. Ryder loves you more than life itself." Her tone turns forlorn on a dime. Is this part of her being stressed or is something else going on?

"Miranda, are you okay? You don't sound like yourself."

"Yeah. No. It's nothing. Don't listen to me. I get a little crazy when I'm this stressed. With you and Ryder taking the planning pressure off me, I'll be able to breathe again."

"Mir, I don't mean to pry, but if you change your mind about getting married, you won't hurt my feelings. I want you to be happy, so if this guy isn't for you, I'll support your decision to back out all the way."

"Thanks, Liv. Your support means a lot to me. But I don't have any doubts about him. Listen, I have to go now, but call me later so we can finish talking about your new business and what else you need from me." She disconnects, leaving me confused regarding my next steps.

Mom walks in a few minutes later, and we spend the next hour preparing our questions before the big meeting. As we talk, brief glimpses of old memories flash in my mind. They're of Mom and me spending time together when I was young. There was a time when I felt her love, felt important to her, and wanted to be with her.

Time stole those memories from me when we grew apart and new memories pushed them out of the way. Now that we've reconnected and are both actively working on improving our relationship, I can relax and enjoy spending time with her again. It feels good to have her advice and business acumen to help guide me. We settle into a comfortable groove and tackle the latest challenge together.

Ryder walks in at the end of our meeting, all smiles and cocky demeanor. "That sounded promising. I'm impressed with both of you ladies. Think you can takeover negotiations for moving into our new house now?"

"We got it? Already?"

"Our offer was accepted within hours of Grady submitting it. Now to sell our two places and move all our belongings. No big deal, right?"

After Mom leaves, Ryder and I decide to go out for a celebratory dinner. Getting the new house with enough land to expand our Mason Creek wedding services was unexpected this soon, but most everything else that's happened to us lately has been the same unexpected whirlwind. One thing the last year has taught us both is to be flexible and adapt to the changes. Our Italian dinner hit the spot, and we opted to enjoy the crisp fall night air by dancing a little at our favorite pub.

When we walk into Pony Up, Faith, Charlee, and Justine are standing at the bar, waiting for their orders. Faith turns and takes a long, hard look at me. Her eyes bug out and her mouth gapes open. Just as Tucker takes a break from singing and the music stops, Faith finds her voice.

And it's uncharacteristically loud.

"Oh my God, Olivia Anderson-King. You're pregnant and you didn't tell me?"

CHAPTER 20

Ryder

Between prenatal visits, selling two properties, moving into our new house, and turning the barn into a posh five-star chapel, the last three months have flown by in a blur. Liv is approaching her fifth month of pregnancy, and every day I marvel at the growing swell of her belly.

We wanted to keep our news a secret until now that she's showing, but her best friend took one look at her and knew instantly. With our secret suddenly out in the open, there was no point in trying to deny it. Faith said Liv had a certain glow that only happens to insanely happy pregnant women. She recognized it from when she found out she was carrying her daughter, Hope.

Immediately after Faith so eloquently announced it to everyone in Pony Up, I texted Grayson to give him the good news before he heard it from someone else. I barely made it. Had he not read my text first, I would've been on my best friend's shit list for a day or two.

Over the last few months, he's been a huge help with cleaning out and remodeling the barn with me. We've managed to keep its original beauty and add all the amenities that set it apart from anything else in the area. After working day and night, we're almost ready to host our first client's wedding day.

"Ry, I've gone over and over this checklist for Miranda's wedding. What am I missing?" Liv hands me the printed list then sits on my lap as I look over it.

"Babe, I don't see anything missing. You've covered all the bases. Even her very specific catering order has been reconfirmed. We are right on track and good to go for her big day. I think it's so cool she chose a wedding dress that resembles an all-white Mrs. Claus dress." I leave the paper on my desk and pull her closer to me.

"Don't say that to her or she won't wear it. She wanted people to think of a Christmas angel instead." Liv chuckles as she curls deeper into my embrace.

"No offense, but she missed the mark on that goal by a mile." While Liv's so close, I steal a kiss or two.

"Oh, hush. She'll be a gorgeous bride. Her very

specific catering request was brilliant. She went to London a few years ago and fell in love with having high tea in the afternoon. I think it's a great idea to recreate that trip for her. We should go before I'm too pregnant to travel. Now that Kiwi is settled into her new palace and is comfortable with our parents coming around, we can afford to run away for a week or so."

"Yeah, you're right. I'll have my people call your people to find a week we can both take off. It's not as if we don't have enough to occupy our time right here in Tiny Town, Montana. Then again, after the baby's born, we won't want to go anywhere without her." My hand drops to her baby bump on reflex.

"Pack warm clothes. It'll be cold there too during New Year's week. That's when we're going. I just decided for you. We have a Christmas-themed wedding next week, Christmas is the following week, then a trip to England. If I can find a hotel room this late, that is. We never had a real honeymoon, so this will be our last chance before we're parents. I'm claiming it now." She kisses me before getting up and walking back to her desk.

She's not kidding about our trip and we both know that to be true. Her fierce determination is one of the reasons I love her though. She's impulsive and fearless while being cautious and concerned at the same time. Somehow, she makes the quirky enigma irresistible.

She's probably searching for reservations during the holiday week right now.

"Did you mail all the wedding invitations when you went into town?" She pokes her head over the top of the monitor.

"Yes, ma'am. Just as Miranda asked, the majority of her guests will be local residents. I get the feeling her fiancé is all about the status of being seen in this wedding. He's not listening to what she wants at all. I don't get why she'd insist our friends attend instead of inviting her own."

"Yeah, I tried to question her about that and point out the obvious—it's backward from every other wedding in the world. You keep strangers out, not the people you know. She said her friends wouldn't go through the trouble of getting here, so she wanted the town to come and be part of our new business venture. It's a weak story, but she didn't budge when I pressed the issue." She shrugs and taps the end of her pen against her lips. "Should I pry more?"

"No, babe, I wouldn't do that. She obviously doesn't want to talk about it yet. Just be there for her when she needs a shoulder to lean on. That time is coming, trust me. We can only hope she'll come to her senses before she says 'I do' if he is the problem. Maybe she just has cold feet and we're reading too much into it."

"Maybe." She doesn't sound convinced, and I know she's worried about her friend.

"Hey, I just thought of something else. Did you ever cancel the divorce? We're coming up on the six-month mark any day now."

She meets my questioning gaze with wide-eyed alarm. "No, I didn't do it. I thought you did it. You didn't contact George or Judge Nelson?"

"Nope. We've been moving at warp speed since we returned from New York City, and it just slipped my mind. If we missed the court date, we may have a warrant out for our arrest. Wouldn't that make George's day?" After scrolling through my contacts, I tap George's name to make sure Liv and I don't have a cell with our names on it.

"To what do I owe the absolute pleasure of receiving a phone call from the famous Mr. King?" George's sardonic tone always makes me laugh, even if he's being serious.

"You've probably seen and heard by now that Liv and I are back together again. Officially. We need to stop the divorce proceedings before it's too late. Neither of us remember the date we're supposed to be in court. Can you help us out?"

"I'm sorry to be the one to tell you this, Ryder, but you both missed your court date, so Judge Nelson finalized your divorce as it was filed. I gave my recommendation on the custody arrangement of your bird and he ruled on it."

"You mean Liv and I are already divorced?" His revelation just sucker punched me in the gut. From the crestfallen expression on Liv's face, she feels it too.

"I'm afraid so, Ryder. That's what you both assured me you wanted, isn't it? You've both waited over a year for this day. I would've thought you'd be relieved you don't have to fight anymore."

Dead silence fills the line as my mind and heart attempt to reconcile the earth-shattering news George just leveled on me.

Then George bursts out laughing. For a solid ninety seconds, I listen to his uncontrolled, maniacal laughter.

"That felt so good. Words can't even describe how much I appreciated this little moment we just had. You missed your court date, but I'd already talked to Judge Nelson and asked for a thirty-day continuance. From all the scuttlebutt around town, I had a feeling you'd call me to share the news. Come by the office tomorrow and we'll withdraw the petition to dissolve your marriage."

"George, I don't know whether to kiss you or punch you when I see you next. Thank you for your help. We'll see you tomorrow." I chuckle and hang up when he has yet another laughing fit at my expense.

I move over to Liv and pull her into my arms. "You're still Mrs. King. George just had a little fun with us after all we've put him through. Maybe he'll take that permanent vacation after giving me that heart attack just now."

"Are you kidding me? I'm going to kill him when I see him. My heart stopped for a minute. At least we have the Tahiti vacation thing as our alibi when he disappears." Liv laughs and drops her forehead against my chest. "Now I can breathe again."

"I was trying to figure out how I'd convince you to marry me a second time. Since I used all my best moves the first time, I'd have to find new ways to trick you into saying yes again."

"There's one thing you can count on all the time. I'll always say yes to you."

WE'VE FINALLY SETTLED DOWN AFTER THE INITIAL run on her lingerie. Once the product specifications were sent to the new factory, the production lines ran at full speed to fulfill all the outstanding orders. Liv hired my mom to manage the retail store in town. Her parents oversee the manufacturing processes, working directly with the factory on new orders. Liv's focus is primarily on nurturing the creative side of the business.

I still manage the marketing part of her clothing line, but we make all the decisions together.

Miranda's wedding is today, and Liv and I have been going nonstop to give her the best ceremony we can. We've connected the lingerie business to the wedding planning in some ways, and we have more plans for the future. For Miranda, Liv created a new white bride-themed teddy, complete with a veil, thigh-high stockings, high-heeled house shoes, and a personalized wedding garter for the groom to remove in private. I tried to get her to model it for me before wrapping it as Miranda's gift, but she refused. She muttered something about we don't try on our clients' thongs before giving them as gifts.

"This place looks amazing, Ryder. I can't believe how much you've transformed it from the barn it used to be. Everything looks absolutely perfect for today. I can't wait for Miranda to walk down the aisle and take it all in. The wedding photos will be fabulous." Liv adjusts some of the hanging flower bouquets as we do a final inspection before the town guests arrive.

"Do you think you should go check on Miranda? She doesn't have any of her family here to help her. It's just odd." I can't put my finger on the crux of the issue, but I'm sure she hasn't told us the whole truth about her situation.

"Yes, I think you're right. She did seem more nervous than usual for her evening wedding. She saw the Christmas trees outside and nearly broke down crying just looking at them. When I brought her in the back door, she mumbled something about the candlelight ceremony, but she wouldn't repeat it when I asked her what she'd said. This is what she told me she wanted, so I hope we recreated the vision she had in her mind."

Liv walks off to join Miranda in the back and I make another pass through all the public areas, just in case we missed something on the other ten rounds we've made. As I walk past the groom's dressing room, I overhear Miranda's fiancé, Victor, talking to the two men who came with him.

"Just a few more hours, boys. Not much longer now."

Normally, that phrase wouldn't catch my attention. The happy groom is usually impatient to reach the end of the night and be alone with his new bride. But the typically cheerful, pre-wedding excitement sounds dark and sinister with his ominous tone. I stop walking and glance around, finding no one in the hall with me, and move closer to the door.

"Why do we have to go through all this bullshit? Why didn't you just go to Vegas and get it over with?"

"Think about what you're asking, Monty. With this wedding, we'll have an entire town as witnesses of the happy couple. No one will oppose our wedding." Victor's voice moves closer to the door as he talks, so I make a quick getaway.

There's no apparent threat in his words, but his inflection speaks volumes. I make a beeline to find Liv and share my concerns with her, but a knock at the front door steers me off my path. We locked the building while the wedding party prepared for the ceremony to prevent curious guests from arriving early and snooping the grounds. After a quick glance at my watch, I realize it's time to welcome our guests and get everyone seated before the bride makes her grand entrance.

Grayson and Grady walk in first. They both promised to help direct people since the entire town was invited to the premier event. The three of us alternate showing people to their seats and corralling those still waiting until the chairs are full and the aisles are empty. The low roar of chattering guests fills the room, and they keep each other entertained while I go check on Liv and Miranda. I haven't seen my wife in too long for my liking, especially with the bad vibes I get from Victor. With my feet carrying me as fast as I can move, I reach the bride's suite and knock on the door.

"Ryder." Liv's concerned voice from behind me makes me whirl around.

"Babe, are you okay?"

"Not really. Umm, Miranda asked me to get her bag of small gifts for the servers out of the car. When I came back in, she was gone."

"What do you mean she was gone?"

"I mean, she used to be here and now she isn't. I've looked everywhere she could possibly be, but she is nowhere in this building. We have lost the bride... on our first event. What should we do, Ry?" Her wide eyes and slack jaw are adorable, even if we're both in deep shit.

"I'll do one more pass around the building to look for her. If I don't find her, I'll break the news to Victor. Wait here in case she comes back."

After checking every nook and cranny in this place, I come to the same conclusion as Liv did. We have a runaway bride and a jilted groom, though I can't say that's a bad thing after meeting her ex-fiancé. I knock on the groom's dressing room door and wait for Victor to open it. When he sees me, his stoic expression doesn't change. This man took no joy in promising himself to Miranda for life.

"I'm sorry to be the bearer of bad news, but

Miranda is gone and didn't leave a note or anything. She asked my wife to get something from the car, then disappeared. We've searched the entire building several times. I'm very sorry to say, but it seems she changed her mind."

His face turns blood red, but not from embarrassment. The fire and anger in this coal black eyes are palpable. He balls his hands into fists at his sides and grits his teeth so hard I hear them scraping inside in his mouth. "Thanks. I'll take care of it. Keep the money. Monty, get my stuff. We're leaving."

And with that, they march out the door without so much as a goodbye.

Liv meets me halfway down the hallway with a disappointed expression marring her beautiful face. "I'm really worried about Miranda. I knew something was wrong. You and I both felt it, but she wouldn't confide in me. Now I have no idea where she is or if she's even okay. We have all these people here, all this food, and a beautiful, delicious wedding cake... but no wedding."

"I know, babe. Let's go tell them before the rumors start." I take her hand in mine and lead her through the side door into the sanctuary.

A hush falls over the crowd and all eyes are on us. The preacher looks more perplexed than anyone.

"Thank you all for coming tonight. This night is

special for many reasons, but we do have an announcement to make about a small change in the agenda. The original couple has decided they need to reevaluate their lives before making a lifelong commitment. Instead..." I turn to face Liv and drop down on one knee. "I'd like to ask my wife to renew our vows in front of all our family, friends, and neighbors."

She covers her mouth with her hands. Her eyes grow wide, and tears instantly fall to her cheeks. "Ryder, I love you more than life itself."

Her reply is only a whisper, but the crowd breaks out in cheers and clapping for us.

I push to stand and take both her hands in mine.

"Olivia Anderson-King, I have loved you from the moment I first laid eyes on you when we were in second grade. You walked into the classroom and took my breath away. Even though I was only seven years old at the time, something in me knew you'd changed my life forever.

"We've had our ups and downs, ins and outs, highs and lows, and none of that will change in our years to come. But I promise to love you with the same awe and wonder I felt the first time I saw you and you blew me away. I promise you'll never question my commitment to you or our children. And lastly, I promise to keep making you scream like a female fox in heat or howl like an alpha female wolf during mating season at least three times a week.

"We'll always be fodder for the gossip mill around town, but we'll also always make it entertaining and worth talking about."

More cheers, laughter, and clapping come from the packed house, but my eyes and ears are only for the woman in front of me. She wipes the tears of laughter and emotion from her cheek, then links her fingers with mine again.

"Ryder, you were my first everything—my first friend here, first boyfriend, first love, and you'll be my last. The last man who owns my heart, body, and soul. For the rest of our lives, I promise to be as stubborn as you are, drive you crazy with my off-the-wall antics, and make you cringe because you're never sure what I might say in public. But I'll never give up on you or our family. I promise to rock your world and keep you on your toes, always wondering what I'll do next. The only secrets I'll keep are the ones you ask me to, or if I have a surprise for you and don't want you to know what it is.

"You've been the love of my life longer than not. That will never change. My love for you only grows stronger every day. I will love you forever. You are my past, present, and future, Ryder King. I'm proud to be your eternal queen."

"Now I will kiss my wife." I pull her into my arms, cover her mouth with mine, then twist and dip her while her eyes are closed. She laughs through our kiss before melting into my arms again. After I stand her upright once more, I turn to the packed house. "Everyone's invited to join us in the reception hall for some delicious wedding cake, champagne, hors d'oeuvres, and hot tea. Feel free to help yourselves."

The chapel empties as Liv and I take a moment to thank each person for coming. When we're finally alone, she smiles as she steps toward me. "You surprised me. I wasn't expecting to renew our vows at all, but I loved every minute of it."

"I thought we should give the whole town the perfect excuse to talk about us."

EPILOGUE

Olivia

Spring in Montana brings warmer days, allowing us to finally start to thaw and see signs of life again. One of those signs of new beginnings happened a few minutes ago when my water broke unexpectedly. It's still two weeks before my due date. I've been staring at the puddle between my feet for the last few minutes, trying to make my brain function past the "oh, shit" moment.

"Liv? Where are you, babe?" Ryder calls out through the house, but I can't answer him.

When he appears in the doorway in front of me, all I can do is stare at him with the proverbial deer-in-the-headlights look.

"Babe? What's wrong? Talk to me. You're freaking me out."

All I can do is point to the floor. His eyes follow my finger then he looks back up at me. "Help me out here. Did you pee on yourself or did your water break?"

His teasing smile breaks me out of my mute trance. "We're having a baby now, Ryder. Right now. I'm not ready yet. It's too soon. I can't do this."

He steps closer to me and slides his arms around my waist. "We're ready, Liv. We've been ready. The nursery is painted, and the furniture has been in place for weeks. You've thought of everything well ahead of time. We've been waiting for our little bundle of joy to make a grand appearance. Today's the day, my love. How about we grab your bag, head to the hospital, and meet our baby today? I'll call the doctor and everyone else on our list while we're on the way."

Over the past few months, Ryder has been my constant in this ever-changing world we've created. His dad bought the jewelry store back and has made a few changes of his own to the merchandise. After his world travels, he wanted to add more culture to the display cases. Now he can't keep the customers out. My lingerie, that was such an abomination to some of the town members when I first opened the store, is one of the biggest new clothing line success stories in the business sector. Then the wedding planning and reception venue took on a life of its own, keeping Ryder hopping from day-to-day.

It'll be nice to slow down when we get home with the baby. I'm taking at least the first four months off work to spend that time devoted to my family.

If I don't die of a panic attack on the way to the hospital first.

The first pain hits hard and fast out of nowhere, stealing my breath away. "What was that?" I thought labor pains started easy and built up over time. That wasn't what I expected at all.

"They say every delivery is different. Maybe this means it'll be over sooner rather than later so you'll have an easier time. Let's get your seat belt on so we can get out of here." He pulls the strap across me and clicks me in tight. After a sweet kiss, he closes the door and jogs around the front of the truck.

"We're starting our new adventure today, babe. You can do this, my love, and I'll be beside you every second of the way."

He holds my hand all the way to the hospital in Billings. When the second pang hit, I noted the time so we could tell the doctor how far apart my contractions were coming. When we reach the hospital, they're right at five minutes apart and gaining strength. About the time fear tries to grip me, another contraction hits and my brain decides it's best to simply get this part done and over with.

I agree wholeheartedly.

"Okay, Momma, we'll take good care of you now. Just concentrate on breathing as much as possible through the pain until we get you ready for the epidural. After that, it'll be much easier on you." The nurse with the sweet smile and tender disposition helps me into a wheelchair and carts me away to a private room.

"Ry?"

"Right behind you, babe. They'd need the entire Army here to keep me out."

After all the poking, prodding, and invasion of any privacy and modesty I thought I had, I'm finally able to relax in the bed. The meter spikes with each contraction, but I don't feel a thing. It's wonderful.

Epidurals: Five stars. Highly recommend.

The sweet nurse comes back in my room to check me, finding Ryder lying on the twin bed beside me. "If you're in the bed, I have to see how far you're dilated too. Nurse's rules, doctor's orders. Spread 'em, Dad." She pops the elastic band on her glove.

"I'm up. I'm up." Ryder jumps five feet away from the bed, making us both laugh.

She measures my progress and smiles warmly up at me. "It's time, Mom. The head is crowning, and this baby is pushing its way out. Do you know if you're having a boy or a girl?"

"No, we didn't find out. We wanted to be surprised. We'll be thrilled either way." I reach for Ryder's hand. "Are you ready to meet our baby, Daddy?"

"Absolutely, and I'll never let go." He kisses the back of my hand. "My baby Momma."

Another nurse joins us to lead Ryder to the delivery room while my nurse disconnects the fetal monitor. When she wheels me into the delivery room, Ryder waits with a sterile cap on his head and gown over his clothes. The doctor moves his seat between my legs and tells me when to push. Ryder acts as my cheerleader and my back support, and I bear down as hard and as long as I can each time.

Then the most precious words I've ever heard fill my ears. "Liv, our baby girl is so beautiful, just like her mommy."

The nurse cleans her off and gives her to Ryder. He kisses her cheek and murmurs declarations of love against her skin as he crosses the room toward me. Then he places her on my chest, and I cuddle her against me. Ryder wraps his arms around us both, and we stare at her in complete amazement. The nurse snaps a picture of the three of us huddled together with an instant camera.

"What a beautiful family." She hands the photo to Ryder, and he holds it up for me to see. "What's her name?"

"Ryleigh Elise King." Ryder and I answer at the same time then look at each other.

"Ryder, I'm so in love with her... and with you."

"I love you, babe, with everything I am. You've made me the happiest and luckiest man in the world."

He means every word of it, but I know the truth. I'm the luckiest person who ever lived. Nowhere in the world would I find another man like my husband. Ryder and Ryleigh are the shining sun, and my entire universe revolves around them. Even as I lie here, cocooned in all the love I could ever ask for, I know trials and problems will come in the future because none of us can escape them. We'll cross those roads when we reach them.

No matter what we face, we'll do it together... and that's as perfect as life gets.

Thank you for reading Perfect Excuse! I hope you enjoyed it. I love creating these characters and walking the streets of their little town with them.

If this is your first time visiting Mason Creek, there's so much more to our little town. Don't miss these fabulous books!

Mason Creek, Montana. The perfect fictional small-town. Come on over and join us.

Series link: https://amzn.to/3yWQIdo

From first loves to old flames, this small town is big on second chances and new beginnings.

A picture-perfect postcard town, where everyone feels at home... and everybody under the Montana sky knows your business.

Get lost here... find yourself here.

Welcome to Mason Creek

12 Books by 12 different authors.

Perfect Risk by CA Harms

Perfect Song by Lauren Runow

Perfect Love by A.M. Hargrove

Perfect Night by Terri E. Laine

Perfect Tragedy by Jennifer Miller

Perfect Escape by Cary Hart

Perfect Summer by Bethany Lopez

Perfect Embrace by Kaylee Ryan

Perfect Kiss by Lacey Black

Perfect Mess by Fabiola Francisco
Perfect Excuse by A.D. Justice
Perfect Secret by Molly McLain

FREE WITH KINDLE UNLIMITED — https://amzn.to/3yWQIdo

Let's keep in touch!

Newsletter
Facebook Reader Group
Website

* * *

ALL I WANT

Rod
The Past

TEN MONTHS OUT OF THE YEAR, I'M NINE YEARS older than my sister, Juliana. But for two months, our numerical age aligns perfectly at ten years apart.

Who would have ever believed those two months could end up being a "make us or break us" deal?

"How is she?" Dad asked from Juliana's doorway, keeping his voice low so he wouldn't wake her. He leaned his shoulder against the doorframe with his arms folded across his chest and a worried expression on his face.

"She's had a rough day, but she seems to be resting easier now." My gaze drifted back to my little sister and a swell of protectiveness filled my chest. Unlike other older siblings who resented not being the only child, I welcomed her into the family with open arms when she was born. Being an only child sucked, and I wanted to be a big brother.

"She needs her medicine refilled tonight. If she wakes up sick again, we can't let her get dehydrated. Do we have the money to afford it?" Mom moved to stand beside Dad, but she'd fixed her worried eyes on Juliana.

"We don't have a choice, Debbie. If our bills have to wait, they'll just be late. Don't stress over that, babe. Give me a few minutes and I'll go to the twenty-four-hour pharmacy." Dad turned his head and watched Mom for several long seconds. I remember the scene like it was yesterday because it struck me as so odd. His daughter was the one he should be focused on, yet he stared at Mom as if it he was seeing her for the first time.

"Thank you, Chris. I know you've already had a long day at work. I can go if you'd rather stay home."

"No, babe, I'm okay. I have a feeling your day has been worse than mine." He leaned down and kissed her on the cheek, then disappeared into the other room for several minutes.

Mom took his place holding up the doorframe. That's when bits and pieces of adult conversations I'd heard over the past couple of years started to make sense. Mom was still relatively young, only in her early thirties. She'd married and had me when she was still a teenager. Then Juliana came along ten years later as a big surprise. The strain of holding our little family together was beginning to show in her face.

"I'm leaving now," Dad announced when he reappeared. "I love you." He stroked Mom's face with his fingertips and she instinctively leaned into his touch.

"I love you too, Chris."

Then he walked over to me and motioned for me to stand. When I complied, he wrapped his arms around me and embraced me in a tight hug. "If I haven't told you lately, I just want you to know what a wonderful son you are, Rod. You've had to grow up way before your time, but I'm proud of the man you've become. I love you, son."

"Love you too, Dad."

Careful not to wake her, he leaned over Juliana and placed light kisses on her cheek and forehead. "I love you, my little precious girl." He straightened and turned his attention back to Mom. "She feels warm again. I think her fever is returning."

"We may end up in the emergency room tonight. I'm doing everything I can to avoid it." Mom scraped her hand over her face, fighting the anxiety of a potential hospital bill we couldn't afford to pay.

"Some things can't be helped, Debbie. We all do the best we can." Dad shrugged, but the heavy weight on his shoulders only amplified the effort that simple move took.

When he moved toward the door, Mom sent him out with her usual request. "Be careful, honey, and drive safely."

Dad looked over his shoulder. He wore a forlorn expression and forced a smile as he nodded.

When he didn't return home within the hour, Mom started to worry about him. She began running through the telltale signs of wringing her hands and looking out the window every few minutes for headlights. At hour number two, she called all the emergency rooms around Atlanta, one after the other, asking about a man who might fit his description. But her search was in vain. After a few hours with no word, she called his buddies, profusely apologizing for waking up the ones who answered.

Despite her efforts, she had no luck finding him anywhere. I kept my vigil beside Juliana's bed the entire night, holding a wet washcloth to her head to help bring her fever down. I wiped her mouth when the little fluid she had in her came back up and held her hand to reassure her she wouldn't die on my watch.

Sometime very early the next morning, I fell asleep in the sentinel position beside her bed in case she needed me again. Mom didn't get one wink of sleep, though. She paced the floor until small streams of sunlight broke through the blinds, shedding light on the dining room table. That's when she saw it, the note Dad had left in a place where he knew we wouldn't find it right away.

What lower-middle-class family ate their meals in a formal dining room?

Some people call it a "Dear John" letter. I call it the coward's way out.

Dear Debbie,
I'm sorry, but the life you want is not the life I want.
Please don't look for me.
I just can't do this anymore.
Chris

This was his family.

This was his wife, his son, and his daughter.

He deserted us, knowing Juliana desperately needed that medicine to get well. He did this, knowing Mom needed her husband and his kids needed their father. But *this* meant nothing to him in the end. The life he wanted was out there somewhere, in a place where we weren't. Whatever he was searching for was obviously better than we were. Something waited for him that was more exciting. He had something new that made him want to get up in the morning and come home at night.

We never knew what we did wrong to make him walk out and leave. None of us had a clue. The coward left that bullshit note and didn't bother to even send us a fucking postcard in all the years that followed. I was only fourteen when I was left to help pick up the pieces of our tattered lives. He destroyed everything when he chose the absolute worst time to have a midlife crisis.

As for his whereabouts, I don't know if Mom ever looked for him after she found that note. I sure as hell didn't look for him either. Our grandparents on his side of the family were devastated by his actions. He was still their son, and they loved him just the same, though. Truthfully, that only made me more bitter about the entire situation because that was a direct insult to my worth. That resentment emerged every time they tried to bring up the subject.

Juliana and I went to visit them one weekend when I was sixteen and she was six. Even at her tender age, she understood what Chris had done to us as a family, although she wasn't as aggressive about his betrayal as I was. When Grandma brought him up around me, it always resulted in a showdown.

"Chris is your father, Rod. You should call and talk to him." She felt it was her place to push us back together, always hoping for a family reconciliation. "A growing boy needs to spend time with his dad."

"Are you talking about the loser who left to go buy medicine for a sick little girl then never came back home? Didn't call. Didn't send money. Didn't care if we had food on the table, clothes to wear, or if we were even still alive. Is that who you're calling my father?" I loosely crossed my arms and gave her a disinterested glare.

Her eyes teared up, and she put her hand over her heart, maybe trying to keep it from breaking in two, but my response ended the conversation. At least she never tried to justify his actions. That would've sent me over the edge and she wouldn't have seen me again. When he left, my heart turned to stone. Fitting, since that's also my last name.

Still, Grandma and Grandpa tried to give us hints

or some other small clue as to his whereabouts, hoping Juliana and I would contact him on our own. But neither of us took the bait. By that time, he was dead to me anyway, and I didn't want him to come back or try to make amends for anything. Watching Mom wear herself out to feed, clothe, and keep a roof over our heads during those years had sealed Chris's fate with me.

During the four years after he left us, I did everything I could to help Mom keep us alive. When she worked extra shifts at the carpet mill, I played with Juliana, read her books, cooked her meals with what little food we had, and made sure she took her bath every night. When Mom came home after spending eighteen to twenty hours on her feet, working in a hot warehouse-style building, she somehow still made time to ask about our days, our grades, and our friends. We never felt as though we were a burden or that we came last to her.

Grandma and Grandpa tried to pick up some of his slack. They knew Christmas and birthday presents were luxury items our pitiful little family couldn't afford to waste wishes on, much less spend money to buy. They made sure the major holidays and milestones were covered. On my sixteenth birthday, an old beater car appeared in our driveway and mysteriously never had an unpaid car insurance bill. Then, there was the Dell laptop and printer they insisted I needed so I could do my homework and get into a good college.

While Mom worked and Juliana slept, I studied every computer language book I could find until I could code new programs in my sleep. Technology was growing by leaps and bounds and only seemed to be more promising in the future. That's where I set my sights from an early age. Fueled by vengeance, but determined, nonetheless, I vowed our little family would never struggle again.

Keep reading here: ALL I WANT

AFTERWORD

Dear Reader,

Thank you for taking the time to read this book and visit the fictional town of Mason Creek, Montana. The other authors in this collaboration and I fell in love with this place and the characters who live there. We sincerely hope you love it too and visit all the characters we've created for the full experience.

While I always strive to make every book as realistic and entertaining as possible, I reserve the right to use creative license where I deem necessary in my books. In the case of Ryder and Livvy, Montana does not have the "no sex during a legal separation" rule. However, Georgia ***does*** have that rule, so the requirement is valid somewhere... just not in Mason Creek.

Please don't use this book as your legal guide. It is for entertainment purposes only.

AFTERWORD

Lots of love,
A.D. Justice

BOOKS BY A.D. JUSTICE

Steele Security Series

Wicked Games (Book 1)

Wicked Ties (Book 2)

Wicked Nights (Book 3)

Wicked Intentions (Book 4)

Wicked Shadows (Book 5)

Crossing Lines Series

Fine Line

Blurred Line

Hard Line

All of Me Series

All I Want

All I Need

The Vault Series

Warning Part One

Warning Part Two

Warning Part Three

The Crazy Series

Crazy Maybe (Book 1)

Crazy Baby (Book 2)

Crazy Love (Book 3, Free Short Story)

Dominic Powers Series

Her Dom (Book 1)

Her Dom's Lesson (Book 2)

Covis Realm, Easthaven Crest Series

Cloaked

Deceived

Unveiled

Stand—alone Novels

Saving Grace

Completely Captivated

Intent

Mistletoe Not Required

Immortal Envy

Just One Summer

ABOUT THE AUTHOR

A.D. Justice is the award-winning, *USA Today* bestselling author of several series and stand-alone romance novels in various romance genres, including romantic suspense, contemporary, and paranormal.

When she's not writing, she loves spending time with her alpha male husband in the Northwest Georgia mountains. They're living out their own HEA, frequently on horseback with a dog in tow.

She is also an avid reader of romance novels, a master of procrastination, a chocolate sommelier, a twister of words, and speaks fluent sarcasm. An avid animal lover, she has two horses, three cats, and two very spoiled dogs.

She loves chatting with her readers. You're welcome to stalk her across all social media!

Connect with her online!

Newsletter
Facebook Reader Group

Website

- facebook.com/adjusticeauthor
- instagram.com/authoradjustice
- bookbub.com/authors/a-d-justice
- amazon.com/author/adjustice
- pinterest.com/adjusticeauthor

ACKNOWLEDGMENTS

First and foremost, I want to thank my Lord and Savior for His continued forgiveness of a sinner.

To my husband: You are my forever and ever love.

To ever reader: Each book is personal and important to the author for a multitude of reasons, but YOU are the reason we share our stories with the world. Every time is nerve-wracking, but I always hope my words will touch you. Thank you for your time, feedback, and support. Whether you like, love, or hate the book, know that I appreciate you with all my heart.

To the bloggers: None of this would be possible without your help, support, and tireless sharing of the books you love and your love of books. I love everyone in this great group of people. I can't name one without naming everyone because you've all been so helpful and are wonderful people. Thank you for sharing my books with your followers and helping me reach my goals.

To my PA/PR Guru: Autumn, thank you for all your help and support. You are so very much appreciated.

To my friends:

T.K. Leigh, thank you for keeping me sane, talking me down from my crazy ideas, and rooting me on when you know I'm going to do it anyway.

Michelle Dare, you are simply the best friend in the world. You can never leave me. I'd find you... because I'm better at digging up information than the FBI.

Magan Vernon, our daily chats, laughter, and venting our frustrations are the stuff friends are made of. You are a great friend.

I love you ladies with all my heart!

To my editor: Karen, thank you for taking such good care of my words and being so understanding about my requests for "one more day."

To the Blurb Whisperer: Brittany, thank you for your help and collaboration on the blurb for Perfect Excuse. You are truly a gem!!!

Made in the USA
Monee, IL
07 July 2022